The **Snow
Leopard**
and the
Ibex

The Snow Leopard and the Ibex

Douglas W. Farnell

Previous Edition:

Paperback: 204 pages
Publisher: AuthorHouse
             (August 21, 2012)
Language: English
ISBN: 978-1-4772-5575-9 (sc)
ISBN: 978-1-4772-5574-2 (hc)
IBSN: 978-1-4772-5573-5 (e)

Ordering Information:

For orders and inquiries, please contact:
1-888-375-9818
www.toplinkpublishing.com
bookorder@toplinkpublishing.com

Printed in the United States of America

FOR SARA

There have been a few times that stand out as key turning points marking my life's transitions. These times were vital in maintaining an upward life journey by breaking the inertia of a stagnant career, letting go of associations that were no longer energizing, or ending relationships that were becoming destructive or downward spiraling.

This book is dedicated to Sara, a very special friend, who supported me through my most recent transition, and led me to seek a more creative, fulfilling work life. Most of all, she inspired me to start and complete this story.

IN MEMORIAM

Alan Stewart Hanson

Co-worker, family man, climbing companion, and close friend.

Over many years we conquered summits, fought our way through bushwhacks, suffered buffoons while at our jobs, and relished campfires where we could be ourselves.

All these things we did together, just as I share the triumph of publishing this book with you now.

Wish you were here, Ace.

THE SNOW LEOPARD AND THE IBEX

Snow Leopard (*Panthera uncia*):
Carnivore; top predator; strong, powerful, cunning, fast, ferocious; camouflaged; possessing a mythical reputation. Status: *Endangered / Vulnerable.*

Ibex (*Capra sibirica*):
Herbivore; steady, sure-footed; dedicated to the herd; nimble; boasts long, scimitar-like horns; seeks high, safe refuges with views of the surrounding area; *prey of the Snow Leopard.*

PROLOGUE

Silk Road Archeological Project
Lake Issyk Kul
Kyrgystan
August 1990

On the third day of the dig, Professor Akmadov arranged for them to join a falconry-hunting trip on horseback in the Kyungey Ala-Too Mountains of the Tian Shan range.

"For this you will need your rifles," he said – welcome news to twelve-year-old Giorgi Bakradidze, who had had his fill of sitting by the computer monitors, watching murky images of the divers exploring the submerged civilization beneath Lake Issyk Kul.

"What are the rifles for?" the boy demanded, unable to disguise his eagerness.

"Only for protection," his father answered. But Giorgi saw his smile, under his mustache.

The horses were a sturdy breed and well adapted to higher altitude. Giorgi patted the neck of his mount as it followed their guide up and up. Patches of snow still clung to the slopes in shady spots, but mostly they picked their way through brown-green stretches of grass. As they rode, they took turns holding, then releasing, a golden eagle, which would sometimes return with a small rodent or rabbit in its talons. Already it was a day the boy would never forget.

They continued to ascend, Giorgi on a dark brown mare behind his father on a black stallion. His father remarked, "We were fortunate having professor Akmadov offer us this trip to Kyrgystan, Giorgi."

"Yes, this hunt with the golden eagles was a great idea. Very special"

"I've known the professor for twenty years. Every couple of years he's on an exciting dig like this one, discovering evidence of old trade routes important to Chinese and Asian cultures a couple of thousand years ago."

"Uh-huh."

"Soon we'll get our chance. The administration has asked me to join a faculty team from the university relocating to Sokhumi in the Georgian province of Abkhazia this fall."

"But father, why there? I thought they didn't like Georgians from Tbilisi?"

"The people there have not had a worldly view in historical and cultural advancements, which is my field and professor Akmadov's. It's a great opportunity to show them Georgian achievements and gain many of the innovations from the West."

Giorgi's heart sank as he thought, "Great! Just when I was starting to have fun on this trip I find I get to live in

Nowhereville. Maybe this will be my last adventure before attending university."

At 3,100 meters, the clouds began to lower, and they stopped to eat the lunches packed in their knapsacks. The fog drifting around them made Giorgi shiver with cold and delight as he bit into his sandwich.

Suddenly, his mouth fell open and he was jolted from his disheartening reverie. A movement in the fog, on the heights above him. Something gray and yellowish, proceeding in a crouch. Something predatory. "Father!" he breathed.

Instinctively, the boy raised his rifle, trying to still his shaking arms while the blood pounded in his ears, but before he could do more, his father grabbed the barrel of the gun. "No! Don't shoot!" he hissed. "It is an *irbis* – a snow leopard! Sacred!"

Snow leopard! Giorgi smothered a gasp. He squinted to make out the legendary creature's shape more clearly. And then, as if he had willed it, the clouds lifted, and they saw a second animal bounding away.

"An ibex!" exclaimed his father. "The snow leopard must be chasing it."

The camouflaged cat streaked after its prey, paying no attention to the fascinated audience below. As abruptly as they had appeared, both animals vanished from view, hidden by the boulders scattered across the slope.

It was a long minute before the spell was broken. Then the guide and Giorgi's father were smiling, shaking hands.

The guide gave Giorgi a great thump on the shoulder that almost knocked him over.

"Is good luck," he grinned. "Snow leopard. Is good luck."

"They are endangered," Giorgi's father said. "We have seen what not many people will see much longer. But for many thousands of years the *irbis* have been in these mountains, and the stories will go on."

Later, as the horses picked their way down, the guide and Giorgi's father retold the legends and tales of historic sightings. And when Giorgi lay in his sleeping bag that night, back once again beside Lake Issyk Kul, he didn't spare a thought for the lost Silk-Road village that drew Professor Akmadov and his students here. No, he pictured with all the clarity of a boy's imagination the mysterious, magical creature.

He let me see him, Giorgi thought. And, if he had seen him, could that not also mean that some of the snow leopard's magic had been passed to him? Its grace? Its elusiveness? Its deadly skill?

He smiled to himself and pulled the edge of the sleeping bag higher as his father snored beside him. The golden eagle may have caught its little prey that day, but he, he had caught the snow leopard!

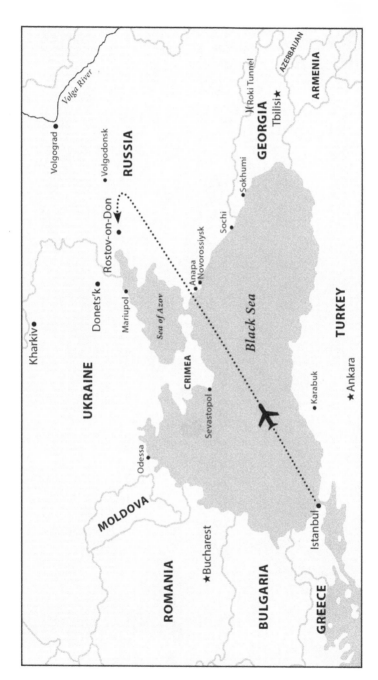

CHAPTER 1
Seeds of Terror

Eighteen Years Later

Terrorist Compound
Karabuk, Turkey
August 2, 2008

Nikolai Sulnikoff, impressed by the tour his two hosts had provided exclaimed, "Well, my first visit to headquarters! So this is where you plan all those nasty surprises for Mother Russia! But how do you keep this place secret? Won't someone see or hear our target practice?"

Giorgi Bakradidze replied to his guest, "Discovery? Not a chance, my friend. The compound cannot be seen from the road, and all shooting practice is done with silencers. And don't forget the constant training of our men!

"Our obstacle courses are in use daily but sounds can't be heard beyond this seven square kilometer space."

"Ahh, I see. But how about entry? Can't anyone come up the dirt road to our location?"

"If they did they would first be met by our 'greeters', three men on duty 24/7, in the trees within ten meters of the main highway, carrying AK's of course. Any stranger would politely be given directions to somewhere else down the road."

"And what if they don't leave?"

"A stronger force would be immediately summoned," smiled Giorgi. "And the intruders would have a very unpleasant experience. We never have to ask twice."

Then Giorgi's partner, Anatoly Buyureck, added, "We've never had any trouble. I purchased this land about four years ago and we built this structure as a parts warehouse as you can see, but allowing for a spacious quarters for the men in the back. We still keep up the pretext of shipping parts to several regular customers in town."

"And you only give tours to people you know," smiled Nikolai, grateful that he had been a confidant and recon specialist for the group for more than two years, even accompanying several terrorist teams on 'mopping-up' operations.

Nikolai knew the training facilities here were in continuous use by Giorgi and his team. And for special ops, the most fearsome men were hand-picked to take on targets in the Russian Federation.

"And I recall that incursion into the rail hub at Krasnodar," said Nikolai.

"Ah, yes," lamented Giorgi. "We were trying for the entire rail complex, damn the luck! A faulty explosive limited our strike to the main control tower and a rail switch. Two killed and two injured.

"But our escape on that rusty freighter to Istanbul was the highlight, thanks to excellent intel from you, Nikolai."

Smiling with a bit of pride Nikolai reminisced, "Always happy to help my comrades out. Lets hope this next target will make up for that disappointment! Speaking of which, I brought some drawings for you to look at, Giorgi," as he unrolled blueprints of an industrial facility with hundreds of pipes and valves.

Nikolai and Giorgi exited to another room in the compound to have a closer look at the drawings. As they did so a short, swarthy, viscious-looking man approached Anatoly and asked, "Is that our reconnaisance guy?"

"Yes, Gustanov," said Anatoly. "Nikolai has been a huge help to us for more than two years now."

"What's in it for him?"

"Oh, it's not just Giorgi and I who hate the Russians, although Nikolai did not lose his parents to military fanatics like we did. Mine, you know, were hauled off to prison in 1984 for not agreeing to share their oil fortune from the Caspian Sea with the Russians and their Dagestani puppets. They were executed shortly afterward."

"Russian *svin'i* – pigs!" Gustanov spat.

"And Giorgi's," Anatoly went on, "were…"

"Giorgi had to watch the damned Abkhazian zealots murder his father and mother in Sukhumi, during the war in 1992," Gustanov added, "while the cursed Russian military advisors looked the other way. Yes, I remember."

Anatoly knew, even without looking at the heaviness of the man's expressions, Gustanov had suffered similar tragedies of close friends in Chechnya, his home country.

Anatoly also knew, as did every man in the terrorist compound, that, fueled by his anger, this man had notched ten kills of Russian soldiers in the bloody Chechen war. He was not someone whose bad side you wanted to be on.

"Come," said Anatoly. Gesturing for Gustanov to follow him, they joined other terrorists who had completed their morning workouts crawling through tunnels, tip-toeing along narrow beams, and ascending ropes on walls, all the while carrying AK-47's or the heavier assault rifles with 30-round magazine capacity. "I think you could use some lunch before your explosives training and studying police reaction strategies in the afternoon. You work hard, my friend, and I must rejoin Giorgi."

Anatoly joined Giorgi and Nikolai in another room and caught the tail end of their conversation: "... yes, that would give us assurance of greater destruction on the ground. And you only need six hours lead time to fully load those holding tanks with natural gas?," asked Giorgi.

"Yes. About 120,000 cubic meters. Should add a nice punch to our calling card. I only have to give my man a signal. He's already accepted half of the $225,000 'gift' and re-routing the gas is a standard procedure during routine maintenance. Even better, he controls the schedule."

"Does he seem eager for the other half of his prize?"

"Absolutely," said Nikolai. I'll be on site with the balance of his payment– in a location, well removed from the strike point, of course."

"Of course," laughed Giorgi. "Ahh, Anatoly, nice of you to join us," motioning for his financier to take a seat.

"Thought I'd drop by and check on progress with our contact at Ataturk Airport," said Anatoly, nodding at Nikolai.

"Looking good," Nikolai responded. "Ozgur is really angry at his supervisor at Ekmek Buk, the airline food service company. And he badly needs the money for his family. I think the $50,000 down payment was the most he's ever seen in his life."

"Money talks," smiled Anatoly.

"And he'll have no trouble covering his tracks as instructed."

Wondering if Ozgur would try extorting them Giorgi asked, "Will he try milking us for more than the remaining fifty?"

"Doubtful," said Nikolai. "I let him know what will happen to his family if he does."

"Looks like no loose ends. Our kind of deal," Girogi smirked. "And the situation in South Ossetia is now at a boiling point with Georgia moving more forces nearer to its northern province. The real fireworks could start any day now."

"And the Americans continue to stir the anxiety of the Russian bear, announcing their intent to move Patriot missles into Poland," noted Anatoly.

Giorgi boldly proclaimed, "I think there will be at least two dozen Russian passengers on board our flight from Istanbul. They cannot resist the leather jackets, silk carpets, and Turkish pistachio at the Istanbul Grand Bazaar and nearby shops. Too many bargains!

"And Ozgur's flight data from Ekmek Bük confirmed an average of thirty Russian passengers per day from Istanbul to Volgograd during the pre-Ramadan weeks in August."

Nikolai reminded his comrades, "Our choice of a Boeing 767 airliner as the strike point will satisfy our objectives. Remember the same aircraft is scheduled to continue to Moscow and Helsinki with no re-fueling required at Volgograd, meaning there will be plenty of fuel to complete our task there."

Nikolai excused himself to rest before dinner leaving Giorgi and Anatoly to review the rest of their bold plan together.

"Do you think Aratanbul's solution will work?" asked Anatoly, referring to the one non-combatant recruit to Giorgi's team who remained in Georgia.

"Yes, I've tested it twice now," said Giorgi.

Their discussion centered around Neomian Aratanbul, a software expert, who created an override of the Boeing 767 navigation system's electronic control protocol.

"I have the software on a small thumb drive in my pocket. It holds the results of two years' work by that old, eccentric computer science professor. I keep it with me always, even while I'm sleeping," he said with a smile.

"I believe your choice of a 767 aircraft was wise, Giorgi. Plenty of fuel for our purpose. A 737 would have been too small."

"Yes, again thanks to Nikolai's research."

"Excellent," replied Anatoly. "And how nice to have Ozgur's help with placement of the weapons.

"It is most fortunate that western policies have stifled terrorist activities for so long that airline security efforts have become sloppy."

"Precisely," echoed Giorgi.

Giorgi seized on the moment, "My friend, our group is nearing its apex in readiness and the world is lining up on the chessboard. I plan to make an announcement after dinner tonight. Time to celebrate."

Anatoly nodded agreement, anxious to hearing Giorgi's oratorial prowess again.

After dinner that evening Girgi rose to address the thirty five followers of his group:

"Gentlemen, you have worked hard to build your skills for our clandestine enterprise. I have watched you for many months as you have gained the level of destructive power of any special forces group in the world."

The men responded with wild applause and cheers, then waited for their leader to continue.

"Our enemy continues to be vulnerable to our attacks and the rest of the world will simply be nervous observers.

"I have chosen to call our group *Irbis,* the Russian and Turkic word for the mysterious and powerful snow leopard of the Central Asian Mountains. I, myself, witnessed this great animal hunting its prey and was awed by its presence. So too, shall the world be awed by our presence and our victory. It is an honor to serve with you in a group with this name.

"Let us celebrate with three drams of whisky."

Emboldened by this speech, the men showed their elation with wild applause and high-fives, as they gulped the liquor being passed around.

Giorgi smiled. "The men are ready. Now is the time for us to meet our destiny and make our mark on history."

CHAPTER 2
Business Woes

⌒✨✨✨⌒

Capricorn Solutions, LLC Corporate Office
Seattle
August 2, 2008

"Hey, are we having this meeting or aren't we? Let's get on it," bellowed Peter Reed, chief operating officer for Capricorn Solutions, LLC, as he tried to form a critical mass for a customer meeting that was long overdue.

"Yes, but we're still waiting for Daniel," exclaimed Linda Kane, company controller. "You know we can't make a decision on this without his okay."

"Yeah, yeah," muttered Peter. "Probably a tiny customer," he mumbled to himself. "If I were running this show no one would be allowed to spend time dealing with this kind of chickenshit!"

"Oh, here he is," said Linda, as Daniel Prescott the company CEO walked into the room. With rugged features Daniel kept himself looking fit with workouts at his club, walking to work every day, and an occasional hike or climb on weekends.

"Hey! Is your sport coat at the cleaners, Daniel?" teased Linda.

"Uh, yeah. I figured it was time," responded Daniel with a smile, knowing his staff liked to needle him about trying to maintain an academic aura with his tweed jacket.

"Must be trying to remind myself I have a Ph.D in computer science," he mused.

His sport jacket was the last vestige of academia. Daniel, who excelled at innovating software applications for higher learning, was also adept at business and managing people. His staff adored him for his collaborative management style.

"Okay, guys. Whatta we got?" said Daniel. "And where's James?"

"I saw him engrossed in a phone call just a few minutes ago," said Linda. "Didn't look like he could come up for air. You know, one of *those* phone calls."

Unperturbed, Daniel switched gears. "Ashley, you know the situation with this new customer proposal, right? Why don't you walk us through the particulars?"

"Be glad to," said Ashley Crowe. "We have a new customer interested in our History, Anthropology, Archeology, and Art packages, with a 'maybe' on our Technology & Science series. Their name is Classroom Colossus, Inc. and their niche is colleges and small universities in the East and Midwest which they're expanding to the West Coast. But it'll be a year before they see results. Academic worlds turn slowly, as you know."

"That's for sure!" Peter said. "And we're adding online functionality that may eventually put some of these 'tweeds' out of work," he noted with a grin using his description of academic types, and to take a playful jab at Daniel.

"How many colleges and universities do they have?" Peter asked Ashley.

"Let's see, small universities, about 36, and about 115 small- to mid-sized colleges," she replied. "They'll soon be a major player in the U.S."

"Hmm. Thanks," replied Peter. Ashley had done her homework. And, as North American sales director, she seemed to understand important words like 'business' and 'profit.'

Daniel glanced at his chief operating officer with an inquisitive expression. "Well, maestro? You had a nicely defined phase-one for the online stuff. Waddya think about a 'Beta' for Classroom Colossus?"

Peter added, "Well, it seems these guys are going places, and their expertise is complementary to ours. They know how to get an 'in' with academic department heads and grad and undergrad student groups."

In fact, both Peter and Daniel believed that online technology would end up *displacing* much of what marginal professorial types performed. There was a technological earthquake poised to rock the stodgy academic world, and Capricorn was positioned to be at the epicenter, with online applications being key.

Carefully thinking of the ramifications, Peter said, "I could have Phase One of the online plan ready after Thanksgiving. But, I gotta have two additional people now! We could be ready to talk to Colossus about a 'Beta' after Christmas."

Daniel was about to wrap up the meeting when James Chin walked into the conference room, looking down at the floor. Daniel had seen that look on his face before, and the news had not been pretty.

"What's up, Doc?" Daniel called out to his marketing director, using his nickname for James.

James looked nervously around the room. "Looks like most people here need to hear this, uh, well, uh, almost everyone…"

Daniel sensed his discomfort and said to Ashley, "Ash, that was a terrific report. Would you call the Classroom Colossus folks this afternoon? Tell 'em we'd like their inputs on a new technology program we're doing and would visit with them in their offices in a couple of weeks. They would have an exclusive for one year. See what their initial reaction is."

Ashley took the hint well and rose to leave the meeting. "I'm on it. I'll advise their response, Peter."

"Thanks, Ashley," Peter said with a rare smile as she left the conference room.

"So, James, what is it? Why the long face?"

"We all know that Helvetia Education, Inc. is our biggest and most profitable customer. Not only that, but we all like working with them, right?"

Everyone nodded.

"I just got a call from their operating VP who apologized in advance but said he has been forced to change their purchasing terms with us."

"Like what kind of changes?" asked Daniel, his stomach beginning to feel queasy.

James glanced at Linda as he continued, "Well, Linda, remember that hour-long instruction session you gave us a while ago about why getting paid on time by our customers matters so much?"

"Right," said Linda. "So what changes are they proposing?"

"They want to pay us in sixty days instead of thirty," squeaked James.

Both Daniel's and Linda's faces drained of color.

"We can't do that!" exclaimed Linda. "We wouldn't be able to expand any of our operations or marketing efforts. All of our expansion capital would be tied up with them. We'd have to get an increase of our existing line of credit at the bank. The impact of their sales volume on our cash flow is so huge."

But James was not finished with his news. "I totally hear you. But Helvetia says there's no negotiating on this."

James didn't need to say anymore. Daniel knew Helvetia had plenty of options to choose from for their software supplier.

"Without them, there would be no way we could keep even half of our thirty-five employees," said Daniel, morosely.

Slowly a look of rage formed on Peter's face. Daniel was quick to spot the impending eruption and grabbed Peter's arm, sliding his chair closer to him. "Easy does it, everybody. Let's think this one through and take the right actions. Better to light a candle than to curse the darkness."

But in that brief moment Daniel knew the future of his company had just been significantly threatened. This crisis would require his immediate attention, and all the discussion of plans with Colossus would have to wait.

James left the conference room and Daniel huddled with Linda and Peter. "Let's call Tom at the bank and see if he's inclined to give us a $1million expansion of our credit line. After all, we've grown annual sales from $1 million to $15 million in four years."

"And our banking covenant compliance and ratios have been squeaky clean for years," said Linda. "But, the banks have been hit hard lately with all this financial crisis stuff. They've cut back on a lot of commercial lending!"

Daniel put the phone on in speaker mode and direct dialed Tom Cable, VP of Commercial Lending at Cascade Summit Bank. A female voice came on the line, "This is Cascade Summit Bank. May I help you?"

"Yes. This is Daniel Prescott at Capricorn Solutions. We're a customer of Tom Cable's. Is he available?"

"I'm sorry but Tom is no longer with the bank. May I connect you to someone else?"

Daniel, Linda, and Peter gave each other that surprised look reserved for greeting someone from Mars.

Linda was the first to speak, "Ahhh, when did Tom leave the bank? This is a surprise to us."

"Just last Friday," was the reply. "May I connect you to his former supervisor, William Blake, who is taking over his duties?"

Linda groaned internally, "Oh, swell. Blake always seemed to be a roadblock every time they wanted an expansion of their credit line."

"Yes, please," she responded.

"Just a minute, please."

The three Capricorn managers continued to exchange looks of fright as they waited the long two minutes for William Blake to pick up the phone.

"Blake here," came the terse voice at the other end of the speakerphone.

"Ah, Bill, this is Linda Kane at Capricorn Solutions. We've just learned Tom is no longer there. Is that right?"

"Yes," was the reply, with no other explanation, as if the rest of the world should accept his one-word dictums and then do as they're told.

"Bill, this is Daniel Prescott, CEO. Why did Tom leave?"

"Well, we were asked to cut our overhead spending way back due to expected higher capital ratio requirements coming from the Feds. I regret having to let Tom go. He was my best commercial banker. I had to let go 70% of my commercial banking staff, and I held on to Tom the longest I possibly could. Orders from above."

"I see," croaked Linda.

"I'm sorry, guys. No one saw this coming. You are my highest-quality customer. Tom always had good things to say about you. I will commit to holding your line capacity to where it is now, but I simply can't do any expansion for any of my commercial banking customers. None. Also, I'm being forced to spend more of my time actually doing hands-on tasks with customers like yourselves."

Blake went on for several more minutes but the three Capricorn executives had heard enough. They knew it was pointless to point out their largest customer had just put the squeeze play on them. It would only spook Blake even further.

Daniel tried to sound hopeful, "Thanks, Bill. Appreciate all you're doing for us. I or Linda will stay in touch." The drone of the phone line meant Blake had terminated the call on his end.

Daniel began to look pensive, but Linda brought him back to reality. "Daniel, my sense is, this crisis is endemic to the entire commercial banking industry. Remember, Fed requirements apply to all banks. They're all going to have to increase their capital ratios, which means they'll be able to lend less. I'll bet several million small businesses in the U.S. will be affected by this. And small businesses do seventy percent of all new hiring! This is going to cause an across-the-board slowdown."

Daniel began to slump further down in his chair, his usual posture when there seemed like no solution.

Linda continued, " Hey, I'll do some checking with contacts I have at other banks in town. The ones who are always trying to get our business. First thing tomorrow. I'll let you know what happens."

"Good idea, Linda. I'm going to try something else. I'll see if Tarkan has any pull with Anatolia Bank, in Istanbul. Since we own half of that enterprise, that could be a source of funds for us as well."

Tarkan Kirni was Daniel's business partner in Istanbul who covered the academic markets in Eastern Europe and the Middle East. It was not a big operation, but it gave Capricorn a toehold into the rapidly-developing Turkish market, which was always eager for American-based education software. Tarkan's company, Bilgi, LLC, also did a small amount of translation contract business for education tools from English to Turkish.

Daniel returned to his office, reached for his land-line phone and dialed the international number for his Istanbul partner.

"Tarkan? *Merhaba! Nasilsiniz?* Hello. How are you? How is your family? Yes, that is good. Glad to hear it."

After a few more pleasantries Daniel came right to the point, "Ahh… Tarkan, you know of the financial crisis that has affected the entire world, mainly because of the actions of the big Wall Street financial institutions? The problem is, we can't get an expansion of credit from our bank to offset the impact of the temporary cash shortfall.

"We're trying all of the banks in Seattle to see if we can make an arrangement, but all of them are affected by a growing unease of supporting too much debt. They can't expand their lending either, especially to small customers. We were wondering if we applied jointly with you we might have some luck with Anatolia Bank in Istanbul."

"Ah, I see," replied Tarkan. "Yes, yes. Yes, my bank, Anatolia Bank. Is very good. Yes, I think they listen to us. Perhaps you come here and we both make request to them. My banker, Tarik Dagci, he is *murdur*, vice president, and is very good. The bank mostly do what he say. When can you come?"

Everyone in the Seattle office thought his informal speaking style was hard to follow, but it tended to add humor to everyone's day.

"Well, this is encouraging," said Daniel. "Yes, I will fly to Istanbul in the next few days. I'll bring our financial statements and projections and some data on our joint projects. I'll send you details by email. And Tarkan, because of this problem, I'm afraid I might not be able to do our climb in Switzerland later this month."

"*Hayir*. No! *Boktan!* Bullsheet!" bellowed Tarkan. "We have plans! We have air and hotel! We both in shape for climb. You can do it!"

"Afraid not, my friend. There are a lot of things I'll need to oversee immediately after returning from Istanbul and visiting your banker. I have to make sure our other clients don't pull surprises like this on us. It's critical for the success of the business. And I have thirty-five employees to worry about."

"Ahhhh *Bok*! Sheet," was all Tarkan could say.

"Okay. See you in a couple of days. *Gule gule*. Goodbye."

"*Evet*. Yes. *Gule gule*. You send email," replied Tarkan, sounding very disappointed.

Daniel reflected, "I never thought I'd have to use financing from Istanbul to keep things going in Seattle. But, stuff happens. Thank goodness the Turkish economy avoided a lot of the derivative shenanigans of Wall Street. I wonder what the other ten million small businesses in the U.S. are doing?"

But as he leaned back in his chair, an familiar wave of anger began to build within him. How long had it been since he'd wrestled with this disturbing feeling, driven by totalitarian forces arrayed against him? In the past it was his demanding, ex-military father. Today it was the abuses of Wall Street banks that denied him, and millions of other small businesses, the credit to expand company programs and hire more workers...

Just as Daniel turned sixteen he became fascinated by computers. He spent much of his spare time with hardware and software publications, thrilled at their descriptions of re-inventing the information world. But within a month he couldn't find any of the magazines he'd saved! He discovered his father had thrown them away, wanting his son to concentrate on military strategies which Daniel hated. Worse, his father insisted on him excelling at martial arts and military discipline at weekly Boy Scout meetings, sponsored and staffed by the local National Guard post.

And then there was his father's demand that he try out for football, becoming a third-string linebacker who was pummelled by bigger first-string linemen in practice.

His frustration grew to the boiling point ...

"Daniel!" boomed Peter, breaking his painful reverie. "We gotta talk." Peter walked in and closed the door.

Daniel spoke first. "I just talked with Tarkan in Istanbul. He thinks we have a good chance to get some financing with his bank. I'm flying back there to make a pitch to their bank along with Tarkan. If we can even get half of the million Linda is talking about, we should be able to squeak by."

"Maybe, but it pisses me off we have to be put in this position because of screw-ups by the financial industry. They even had to lay off Tom Cable! And forcing us to the wall. Now our expansion plans have to be put on hold because we can't get external capital! We'll have to throw that whole Classroom Colossus thing out the window. Thanks a lot, assholes of Wall Street!"

"Now, Peter. No need to go off the deep end." "Now's the time to keep cool about this while everyone else is panicking. If we do, we may have an advantage."

"Daniel, dammit! You gotta be more aggressive with these bankers! Why don't you get more angry with these guys? Ashley says its because you're really into meditation and can deal internally with anger issues."

"Well I guess I'm not comfortable getting all riled up. It reminds me of when my father got angry. Neither my mom nor I could deal with him afterward. I went to meditation training when I was a teenager and it helped me get centered and better able to understand and control stressful situations."

Peter continued, "I've been doing a lot of reading about this financial mess. The big Wall Street banks are the ones who've screwed up the entire financial system, so who ends up getting hurt the most? Them?

"Of course not! It's us! Small businesses!"

"Peter, I agree with you," interjected Daniel. "No question. It's an unfair accumulation of corporate power. Just like back in the days of John D. Rockefeller and Standard Oil. Only then we had a democracy that knew what a disastrous distortion of capitalism that was and broke up those huge monopolies and oligopolies."

"Exactly! We knew how to kick ass back then," replied Peter, sensing his boss was beginning to see the light. "Now our elected officials are controlled by huge sums of money from these freakin' lobbyists."

Daniel knew Peter was right and also knew he could go on playing this blame game until the cows came home. "Peter, you're right. Today is Friday, and it's likely I'll get some work done over the weekend so I can visit with Tarkan's bank next week. I should be back the following week."

"Yeah, you're right, boss, as usual." Peter had finally expelled most of the venom he had been holding back.

"Look, man. You gotta hold it together now. You're the one guy I trust who knows the whole show and has a good business mind. You have the con until I get back. Linda will handle anything financial.

"We'll get there."

"Okay, boss, if you say so." Peter was returning to his normal analytical mode. He turned to give a final goodbye as Daniel headed out the front door. "And, Daniel—"

"Yes?"

"Please get rid of those tweed sport coats. They make you look like you belong in a lecture hall on campus."

Daniel laughed. "Okay. If we're successful in arranging adequate financing, I'll ditch the tweed sport coats forever."

"Promise?"

"Yep! Promise!"

Starbucks Coffee, Top of Queen Anne Hill
Seattle
August 2, 2008

Just after six in the evening, Daniel arrived at his favorite place to meet Arianna Reynolds, his close friend of three years. He spied her sitting at a window table nursing a coffee, a backpack at her feet with her workout gear partially hanging out the sides. She stood to greet him with a hug.

"Long day?" she inquired.

"Yeah. This one was a doozy," said Daniel. "One for the record books."

Intrigued, she asked a couple more questions and Daniel related the major issues of the day, including his decision to travel to Istanbul to see Tarkan.

"Wow, you really had a tough one. How is Tarkan?" she asked.

"Oh, he's fine. Just disappointed we won't be climbing this." He handed her a small photo of the Matterhorn taken from the town of Zermatt, Switzerland. It was his favorite view of the mountain and he usually carried a couple of 4x6 copies as a conversation starter.

"Yes, that must be a blow for both of you. I know how much you like climbing together."

Arianna Reynolds was the type of woman no one could ignore. Tall, slender, blonde, with an oval face and high cheekbones, she instantly caught most men's attention.

Most people would have been surprised to know that, at thirty-eight, she had never been married. But Daniel knew about some of her previous relationships and that men were always so absorbed in her beauty that they never explored beyond it. He was one of the few men who did so and delighted in knowing her inner qualities: a calm energy, a curiosity for many things in life, a capacity to express great joy, unreservedly at times, and an ability to laugh at herself.

They pursued activities together that varied from symphony concerts and ballet, to hiking, kayaking and snowshoeing.

Her success as a communications manager for Cedar Stream Architects reflected her high emotional intelligence.

Just before they rose to depart, Arianna reached over and squeezed Daniel's hand. "You be careful," she commanded. "Don't get into any grand adventures! Remember the Good Guys motto: just get in there, get the job done, and get the heck home."

Both of them laughed at the way she liked to tease him about the limited way most men viewed work in general.

But, while laughing with her, Daniel was temporarily stunned. Her touch had reminded him how much they had become such integrated parts of each other's lives.

As they rose to leave Starbucks Daniel inquired, "Why don't we have a glass of wine at my place? Just a block away."

Over Cabernet Sauvignon they chatted about his upcoming trip and Arianna playfully warned, "Don't forget to stay away from those belly dancing parlors in Istanbul!"

"It would take a lot of belly dancers to make me forget about the night we spent together after last year's Christmas party."

Arianna's face turned red and she mumbled, "Oh, I don't want to talk about that right now."

"You're right, we didn't fully know what we were doing. It was probably a mistake."

Temporarily uncomposed Arianna tripped over a box next to the sofa and its cover came off, "Ooops, wasn't watching where I was going. Hey...what's this?" holding up what looked like a Kung-Fu outfit. "I didn't know you were a martial arts expert!"

"Oh, that's from a long time ago. I was just going to throw it out. It reminds me of karate and weapons training, military strategy and hand to hand combat drills. Things

I'm not proud of. I hated doing them but was forced to by my father who would be checking with all of my instructors about my progress."

"Uh-huh, I see." Realizing Daniel was getting into a sensitive part of his past she asked, "Were you able to get out of that situation?"

"With difficulty. When I was sixteen I had finally had enough. I hid at a friend's house for three days, and refused to return home unless the boy scout and football requirements were dropped."

"Good for you, knowing when to stick up for yourself."

"My mom and dad argued for the three days, mom threatening to divorce him unless he relented. Finally my father gave up. But things were never the same between us. He would avoid me most of the time after that."

"That must have been tough."

"It was, but then I had time to do things I longed to do, especially building computers and attending math club. I enjoyed programming and was delighted whenever there was a new technical break-though."

"And you excelled at computer science in college, right, *Doctor* Prescott?"

"Yeah, and look where I am now," he smiled. Developing educational software and working with fun people."

"I had no idea you were trained in all that military stuff."

"Well I had to learn it, but I doubt I'll be using it again."

"Well at least I won't have to worry about you taking care of yourself," said Arianna, smiling.

"You never know when I might have to," he grinned, recognizing Arianna comments had drawn him out of his painful memories.

Then, remembering he had a goodbye gift for her, he took her hand and placed an object in her palm..

"I got this for you today. Just a little reminder of our friendship over the past three years. Here, I'll put it on your pack." He grabbed her backpack from the floor and attached the pin to its back flap. It was about two inches wide, a bull, Taurus, Arianna's sign of the Zodiac, symbolizing patience and reliability, a loving nature, and serenity.

He showed her a second pin while sticking it on his sport coat. It was an ibex, a member of the Capricorn family and his Zodiac sign, as well as his company's logo. It signified steadfastness, dedication to the cause, and sure-footedness in precipitous terrain.

"These are really cool. Where did you get them?"

"At the Pike Place Market. I decided to take a small break after all the crises happening today and walked down there before coming to the coffee shop."

Before she could gush any more he gave her a big hug. "I'll be careful, I promise. And I should be back in about a week."

She returned the hug and wished him well. Then Arianna left his condo and strode off into the warm evening, giving him a playful wave as she walked away.

CHAPTER 3
Guns of August

⌒≈⦂⦂⦂⦂⦂≈⌒

Terrorist Camp
Karabuk, Turkey
August 8, 2008

Giorgi and Anatoly were reflecting on their success one evening, when one of the men excitedly interrupted them with news that Georgian forces had begun an invasion of their northern province, South Ossetia, where several thousand Russian "advisors" were stationed.

The three men rushed to the nearest TV set and heard the newscaster...

"...The Georgian objective was to destroy South Ossetian and Russian forces and capture the city of Tskhinvali, a preliminary move toward controlling the Roki Tunnel, the primary transit point from Russia through an impassible part of the Caucasus Mountains..."

Giorgi realized now was the time to mobilize his team. With the Russians preoccupied with an invasion of Georgian provinces a bold strike into the Russian heartland would carry a maximum leverage of fear.

The stage had been perfectly set to inflict a weapon of destruction on Russia for which there was no defense: *Terror*.

Giorgi called all his men into the large dining room and turned on the large TV to a station broadcasting in Russian, giving more details about the invasion.

The TV announcer rambled on about more military logistics, but Giorgi had already turned away from the monitor, even as his men continued to watch. He was ecstatic.

The Russian – Georgian War of 2008 had begun!

Giorgi nodded at Nikolai who proceeded to make a phone call to his contact in Volgograd…

CHAPTER 4
Growing Awareness

⚜

Green Lake
Seattle
August 8, 2008

Arianna, feeling that there was more to know about Daniel's trip and his business predicament, called her close friend Joan and arranged for the two of them to meet at Green Lake, a popular walking and jogging location in Seattle's north end. Joan sensed Arianna was beginning to wrestle with something new.

On a hunch Joan asked, "So were you able to see Daniel off this morning?"

"Uh, well, no. But I did say goodbye last Friday. He called me on Sunday to say he had difficulty getting the best plane reservations to Istanbul and wouldn't be leaving until Wednesday, arriving in Istanbul this Thursday. Which way do you want to walk today? Clockwise or counterclockwise?"

"Counter."

The two women set off to circle the lake, as they did every Monday morning before work. Arianna was unusually silent, contributing only an occasional monosyllable, and not even noticing when a jogger coming the opposite way slowed to a crawl to look her up and down.

Joan snorted. "How is it that, even when you're in sweats and not wearing any make-up, guys do that to you? What am I, chopped liver?"

"Hmm," mumbled Arianna.

"And why aren't you talking this morning? Earth to Arianna! Is this about Daniel?"

That stopped Arianna in her tracks. "What are you talking about?"

Joan kept right on walking, and her friend had to scurry to catch up to her. Joan was the only one who knew about the one-night stand Arianna had with Daniel a year ago. Even though it didn't lead to anything more romantic Joan reminded her recently that her deep friendship with Daniel had continued in a very healthy way.

"Well, when you're quiet like this you're usually preoccupied with a guy," says Joan. But you and Jerry the Jerk broke up weeks ago, so unless you're having second thoughts about him—"

"No," Arianna interrupted, with a shudder. "That relationship went nowhere."

"Exactly," said Joan. "So that leaves Daniel. You were thinking about Daniel."

"Daniel is not just a *guy*," Arianna protested. "I mean, he is, of course, but I don't think of him that way. In a relationship way. Like Jerry or Mark or—or—"

"Or Whatshisname," put in Joan. "Don't forget Whatshisname, who got mad that you wouldn't sleep with him after he took you to that trendy restaurant?"

"Or him," agreed Arianna, rolling her eyes. "Daniel isn't one of *them*. He's a friend."

"Uh-huh."

"He is!"

"Great."

Arianna grabbed her friend's elbow to stop her. "Daniel is a friend," she repeated. "I was thinking about him—I admit it—but only because he has all these business worries, and then there's this trip to Istanbul..."But he's not relationship material. He's always been so low-key. Except, the weird thing is, he had this crazy, militaristic dad who made him do all these Rambo things when he was a kid. Can you imagine? Daniel doing martial arts and football and learning to shoot? Who knew? Sometimes I wonder how he runs his company so successfully, being so soft-spoken and all."

"You can say that again." The two women stood aside to let by a woman pushing a double jogging stroller. "You prefer the macho types who are only interested in sex, or parading you around on their arm for eye candy."

"Joooannn!" Arianna protested, admonishing her friend for hitting a little too close to home. "I have everything I want. A great middle management job, a good salary, a nice condo..."

Joan decided her friend had yet to see the bigger picture of relationships and decided not to press further. "My goodness, the time! I must be going! I have a client in fifteen minutes!"

As they neared the parking lot they were approached by an old, homeless woman begging for money. Arianna fished a dollar bill from her pocket and handed it to the woman who smiled weakly then wandered off.

Joan pressed her friend, "Why do you give them money? You know they use it for drugs!"

Arianna, looking wistful, replied, "My grandmother was homeless after her husband left her. She had no job skills and died an old woman, while sleeping under a bridge."

"Oh, I'm sorry to hear that. Is that why you've placed so much importance on getting a well paid management job?"

"Yes...," said Arianna coming to tears.

They hugged. Joan added, "It's okay to have that as a motivator. You've done very well for yourself."

Arianna realized her friend had just offered examples of her professional savvy about relationships.

"Love you. See you soon," Joan called back to Arianna.
"Absolutely."

CHAPTER 5
Istanbul

~~~∽

Istanbul, Turkey
August 8, 2008

Daniel had arrived in Istanbul the prior day and had begun discussions with Tarkan after taking half a day to recover from jet lag. They spent the remainder of the day creating an analysis and presentation for Tarik Dagci, the vice president at Anatolia Bank that Tarkan recommended.

When they arrived at the bank on August 8, Tarkan asked a bank receptionist, "Is *murdur* Dagci available?"

"Oh, he is in Volgograd, Russia, visiting prospective clients. May I assist you in some way?"

"*Bok*. Sheet!" Tarkan cursed, internally. Then, regaining is composure, he asked politely, "Why is he in Russia?" The receptionist, who appeared very familiar with Dagci's schedule, replied, "Mr. Dagci is pursuing a number of inquiries from companies wishing to do business connected with the build up for the 2014 Winter Olympics in Sochi. There are several Russian and Eastern European firms wishing to take out loans for this business opportunity."

Tarkan related to Daniel: "Everyone go crazy trying for construction project bids. Need western equipment or western subcontractors. Even when Olympics are six years away, they must make deals, then plans, then build. Financing from western banks are best way to get these things. That why they want Anatolia Bank. I told you Tarik was good! Everyone want him to handle their deal!"

"Can you ask when he will return?" asked Daniel.

Tarkan checked with the receptionist then related to Daniel: "At least two weeks until he return to Istanbul."

"Oh, that's way too long," groaned Daniel. "We can't wait. Ask if we can make an appointment with him this week in Volgograd. Say next Monday."

"You crazy, Daniel? We fly to Russia for a loan?"

"It's our best shot," remarked Daniel.

"Okay. I ask."

Tarkan was able to secure a two-hour time slot at 10:00 a.m. that coming Monday with Dagci in Volgograd. That gave them two days to make travel arrangements. Daniel agreed, and Tarkan took down the contact and location information. The two partners left the bank and headed to the square at the Blue Mosque to get some air.

Daniel remembered Peter commenting about this intriguing Turkish city of 8.8 million. "Istanbul, the New Paris," Peter had called it. Turning to Tarkan, Daniel said, "How about seeing a few of the sights while we have some time?"

"Sure, no problem."

After munching on lamb kebab; *zerde*, sweet rice with saffron; *helva*, crumbly cake; and *baklava*, Tarkan took Daniel inside the famous Blue Mosque for a visit between prayer services. Daniel was awed by the cavernous mosque, with six 100-foot tall minarets surrounding the elaborate architecture of the main building.

"When we return from Volgograd, we visit Topkapi Palace and the Hagia Sophia Mosque. Each can be full day but we do 'Tarkan Tour,' allow time for lunch and café. Now, on way to boat trip up Bosporus, we go through famous Grand Bazaar. You not gonna believe this place. Bazaar have roof and is twelve acres size. It have everything from Asia and Europe you imagine.

"Now, one more stop before Bosporus." He directed Daniel a few blocks farther into the old town district, not far from the Blue Mosque.

"Here is my friend's rug shop. Only reason I show you is he has best carpets in town. Come from Turkey, Iran, Uzbekistan, and Azerbaijan. He deal directly with weavers. No middlemen. And he take credit cards, *and*…his rugs are half the price you pay in U.S., and he include shipping to USA in his price. Is easy deal."

Uh-oh, thought Daniel. Another friend of Tarkan's. Looks like I'm going to be taken for a ride again! Maybe I should give it a whirl. And, since these rugs last a couple of lifetimes, this is really an *investment*, not an expense."

"Here is his shop, Noah's Ark Carpets and we are in Ticarenthane Sokak," announced Tarkan. "Best in business. Don't worry, he knows you are my friend. I make sure you get best deal. He don't give me *boktan*, bullsheet!"

Daniel and Tarkan entered the carpet shop, and as Daniel inspected the huge selection of rugs and kilims he was amazed at the colors, patterns, and quality of the weaving. Many rugs had stories of events or animals or special symbols built into the patterns, as if the weavers were describing activities from centuries ago.

"*Allah, Allah*! Oh my God! Daniel look at this! These patterns show dogs used to protect sheep from wolves. The weavers show their respect for these animals protecting their wool supply. Remember, many weavers live in mountains where grasses are greenest and good water. Give best wool. These are special rugs. You like this one, Daniel?"

"Yeah," replied Daniel. "I really like the deep reds and blues. And these patterns make it look like a mirage, almost like a dream!" Daniel remained fascinated by the image of a large cat-like creature and asked Tarkan if he could find out if there was a story behind it. Tarkan spoke for a moment with the shop owner and translated the response to Daniel.

"The cat was snow leopard," related Tarkan. "Because grazing pastures sometimes high in mountains, snow leopard take one of the weaver's sheep." The rare encounter with the almost mythical cat was captured by the weaver in this carpet design. Intrigued, Daniel recalled the snow leopard was a natural predator of mountain goats and ibexes. Daniel nodded toward Tarkan signifying his interest in buying this rug.

Other thoughts came to Daniel's mind.

"Tarkan, remember that climb of the Taschhorn near Saas Fee, Switzerland,? We came upon an ibex near the summit?

Just before attempting the final push to the top, they had spotted the animal on a narrow rock outcropping. They were amazed by its agility, how it could casually shift from tiny ledges to knife-edge ridges.

"Yes, seeing snow leopard in carpet make you dream story," remarked Tarkan. "Seeing is dreaming! Here, I get best price for you." Tarkan began to negotiate with the owner, but took a quick break to mention another rug that caught Daniel's interest. "That one has silk woven in with wool, a Tabriz. Persian rug. Is softer and last even longer. I negotiate for both. Get better price that way for each."

Several minutes later Tarkan exlaimed,"Good," said Tarkan. "You get great deal. Don't worry. I have him ship everything to office in Seattle. Is included in price. You lucky guy."

Their shopping business concluded, Tarkan called his office, "Make airline reservations for myself and Daniel to Volgograd, Sunday morning. No! I don't care if we don't sit together. We must depart Ataturk before noon." The flight on Sunday was nearly full but his assistant was able to secure two non-adjacent seats on Karaca Airlines.

The two men departed the rug shop and took the tram to the Golden Horn waterfront where they boarded the boat for an evening cruise up the famous Bosporus Strait.

Daniel marveled at the exotic waterside residences lining both sides of the straight, like Kasbahs for modern day Sultans. "I'll bet these people sure know how to throw parties!" he exclaimed, eliciting a smile from Tarkan.

"Oh, Yes, my friend. I've heard stories you wouldn't believe," waving his hand as if just burned himself.

As evening fell, they returned to the Golden Horn and headed for dinner at a restaurant in nearby Sultanahmet, with delicious seafood creations that drew praises from Daniel.

"Daniel," said Tarkan,"I wanted to tell you of my recent climbing adventures."

"Yes, please do."

"To stay in best shape I join climbing club and make summits in eastern Turkey and Caucasus."

"Excellent. What were the highlights?"

"We climb Mt. Ararat in eastern Turkey, 5,137 meters or 16,854 feet."

"Wow, that is higher than the Matterhorn! Too bad we had to cancel our climb. You would already be acclimatized to the altitude."

"Yes, most unfortunate. The Caucasus climbs completed with climbing club from Russia. I became friendly with members. There was stocky man, name Mustafa. He speak fluent Russian and Turkish with scattered English.

"I can vouch for his excellent climbing skills."

"Sounds like a good guy to have around."

"Whenever we climb Matterhorn I would like him to join us, okay?"

"Yes, of course. Especially since you have climbed with him."

CHAPTER 6
HIJACK!

Ataturk Airport
Istanbul, Turkey
August 10, 2008

The memory of his parents' traumatic murder rushed through Giorgi again, but this time it was accompanied by a flood of power. Like the rare snow leopard about to pounce on its prey.

The *Irbis* team departed from its camp in Karabuk and travelled to a hideout facility about two kilometers from Istanbul's Ataturk Airport where they were joined by Ozgur.

There, after giving his men a five-hour rest, Giorgi confirmed that all key elements of his hijack team were in place and ready to go. He decided another run-through of their cover story would be wise. Testing the men he said, gruffly,

"Gustanov, let me see your papers! And what is the purpose of your trip to Volgograd? Show me why I should believe you're an engineering estimator...". Giorgi repeated this drill with all 5 members of his team, until he was satisfied with their deceptive responses. He authorized Ozgur to report to his work station as flight prep specialist at Ekmek Buk.

In the food warehouse Ozgur pushed a hand cart containing weapons he had sneaked into the facility: several food bins with six Heckler & Koch MP5K submachine pistols, each with fifteen round magazines, six Glock 17 Semi Compact 9 mm pistols, eighteen spare MP5K ammo clips, eighteen spare Glock ammo cartridges, two small C4 explosive packages, six assault knives, and over 200 plastic handcuffs. Each bin had fake seals of approval from the airline security authority on its exterior surface.

"I hope these certification seals will fool any employee and the inspectors from DGCA, the Directorate General of Civil Aviation," thought Ozgur."A lot is riding on this."

At 5:06 a.m. the next morning, Ozgur successfully entered the proper entry code in the food service storage area in the nearby flight-support facility. He placed the bins in the shipping area of the cooler and coded them for that day's Karaca Flight 1025 to Volgograd in the shipping system..

"Whew. It is done!"

As soon as he cleared the premises, he placed a cell phone call with a disposable phone and when Giorgi came on the line, Ozgur gave the signal "Pigs will fly" and hung up. He wiped his fingerprints off the phone and disposed of it several kilometers from Ataturk.

Giorgi nodded to his five-member team.

On August 10, 2008, at 6:15 a.m. Istanbul time, the *Irbis* team commenced its hijack plan.

They entered Ataturk in three separate teams of two, at three different locations spread throughout the massive terminal. Their entrance was three hours before the scheduled departure of 0950 hours, allowing the men time for a relaxed check of the airport before boarding.

Giorgi and Datchi Ackandi, his second in command, made their way through one of three security checkpoints with minimal carry-on gear and aroused no suspicions among the security personnel. "This was the easy part," thought Giorgi. "It would get tricky soon enough."

They were traveling as Turkish construction contractors, each with a modest briefcase containing drawings, spec sheets and partially completed contracts.

Karaca Airlines had recently added this flight to its schedule to service the huge market of Western businessmen, contractors, consultants, and government types. Recently formed out of multiple Turkish airlines that had prior financial difficulties, Karaca had multiple routes in Turkey, Russia, and Eastern and Western Europe.

Giorgi and Datshi waited in the first of two seating areas for KRA flight 1025, scheduled for Volgograd, then Moscow and Helsinki. Giorgi knew only too well what the second area was for. Agents from the DGCA did personal screenings of every passenger boarding commercial aircraft, including personal interviews and additional carry-on bag searches. At one hour before departure, the two men rose to enter the inner seating area for their interviews and security checks.

"Your papers, sir," demanded a loud, short security agent, who challenged Giorgi about his proposed visit to Volgograd.

"Of course," Giorgi replied, even though he wanted to tell this asshole to go to hell.

The two men successfully passed the interrogation part of their boarding and chose adjacent seats in the second lounge section with a clear view of the Karaca Airlines Boeing 767-200, clearly distinguishable by the stylish logo of a small deer on its tail and fuselage. Karaca was the Turkish name for the swift, deer-like animal prevalent in Russia, Turkey, Western and Eastern Europe. While pretending to discuss elements of their construction contract, they observed the loading of the aircraft with baggage and, more importantly, the food storage bins for in-flight meals.

"Ahh," Giorgi said in a low voice to Datshi. "Here we go. There should be a total of fifteen food bins. Remember they are loading for the full trip all the way to Moscow and Helsinki. Five of those bins are ours." His pulse accelerated. Their plan had reached a critical point.

Suddenly, Giorgi caught his breath.

"Kak!" Shit. he cursed quietly as the van section of the Ekmek Buk food services truck began to rise on its hydraulic lifters into the aircraft's mid galley. Four armed men in olive drab uniforms and red berets had casually sauntered into the loading area of the tarmac and eyeballed the ascending food van.

"DGCA," he whispered to Datshi. "Random check." A sickening feeling came over him as one of the men held up his left hand, signaling for the van to be returned to tarmac level.

His thumb hovering over his cell phone keys in case he had to abort the mission, Giorgi decided to let this apparent misfortune play out. One man began opening one of the food bins and examining the contents. Satisfied, he repeated the process on another bin. After a few tense moments, the man raised his arm in the air and made a twirling motion, a signal to re-start loading the plane.

Giorgi gave a low sigh of relief. "Our bins are supposed to be marked 'Dinner' for the later flight leg to Helsinki. They also have a diagonal scratch on the lower right of the identification panel. We should be able to find them easily enough."

Soon, the four remaining *Irbis* team members transited the interview screening and took their seats in the final holding area. When the boarding agent announced, "We will begin boarding first class at this time," Giorgi and Datshi took their place in the first class line to begin their journey into history. They were followed several minutes later by the remaining four terrorists in coach. A few positions behind them were two other men. One was of medium height and Middle Eastern descent. The other was a tall Caucasian with a solid physique and masculine features, wearing a tweed sport coat.

After the aircraft doors were closed, the jet way began to pull away from the wide-body, double-aisle Boeing 767, and the flight crew commenced the engine start sequence. KRA Flight 1025 from Istanbul to Volgograd, Moscow and Helsinki, with a full load of 186 passengers and crew, was under way.

Giorgi and Datshi sat in first class near the galley, Gustanov and another terrorist were seated in the coach midsection, again near the galley. The remaining two *Irbis* team members were located near the rear coach galley.

"It begins, "Giorgi whispered to Datshi. "The *Irbis* is going hunting."

KRA 1025 backed away from the gate and taxied out to the active runway, positioning itself for takeoff. Moments later, its powerful GE CF6-80C2 engines revved to maximum takeoff thrust and the aircraft began its sprint down the runway.

Eight minutes later, when the aircraft had reached 20,000 feet, the hijackers sprung their well-coordinated attack.

With a yell in Georgian, "*Irbis* attack," Giorgi bolted into the first class galley and pinned the two flight attendants together on the floor. Datshi followed immediately and began a rapid search of the 'Dinner' food bins having the telltale scratches. In less than ten seconds, he shouted his success, securing two MP5K machine pistols, two Glock 17 handguns, and two bags of C4 explosive, each containing a small detonator.

Meanwhile Giorgi secured the hands of both flight attendants and stuffed a gag in their mouths, with cord and handkerchiefs from his pockets. He held them prone with his body weight and tied their bound hands to their feet with the extra cord length, completely immobilizing them.

"Giorgi," Datshi yelled, sliding him a Glock and an MP5K, along with a bag containing plastique explosives.

"Got it!" yelled the *Irbis* leader jumping up from his position on top of both women, slinging the semi-automatic weapon around his neck, and grabbing the Glock and plastique. The force of his movement brought a groan of pain from one of the women. The other, a pretty, petite blonde, gagged and her hands bound, could see the comm control, just out reach in the galley.

There were shouts from the passengers who finally realized they were under attack from terrorists. *"I dl k chortu,"* Go to hell, shrieked one woman in Russian. *"Poshol ti na khui, Mudak!"* Fuck off, Asshole, bellowed another man, also in Russian, who made the error of getting out of his seat and approaching the galley.

Covering both entrances to the first class galley with his MP5K, Datshi caught movement coming toward him from a few rows aft of his position.

"Some foolish passenger trying to be a hero," he thought, as he whirled and fired a three-second burst into the floor of the aircraft, just in front of the man's feet.

"Ayyyee," he screamed and immediately cowered against a seat on the port side with his hands raised, crushing another passenger who uttered a muffled cry of pain. There were no further attempts to stop the hijackers.

As soon as Giorgi had the Glock and C4, he leapt forward to the cockpit door, attaching the C4 to the lock-latch. He inserted the detonator into the soft, putty-like material and backed away, thumbing the compact, radio-controlled switch as he retreated.

A loud *"Pop"* confirmed the accurate placement of the explosive and detonator, destroying the door's locking / latching mechanism. Immediately, Gustanov appeared next to Giorgi, having sprinted from the mid-galley, carrying an MP5K and a rubber contraption with two suction cups which had been in his carry-on bag.

"Attach it here and here," Gustanov grunted, pointing to the door. Within seconds the suction cups allowed both men to yank the cockpit door open and Giorgi thrust the muzzle of his Glock into the captain's face.

"You will obey my orders. Don't try to alert anyone," he commanded in English, sweeping the Glock alternately between the captain and the co-pilot. Both Karaca officers were completely surprised by the attack, neither having time to radio in an alert to the Ataturk Regional Air Traffic Control Center, RATCC.

The terrorists in the mid galley had similar success, slugging one of the flight attendants in the face, knocking her unconscious. The other attendant was so terrified she was easily forced to the floor, had her hands and feet bound and her mouth muffled.

The terrorists then recovered all remaining weapons from the food bins.

From his seat in 34F, Daniel became alarmed as soon as he heard the passengers' screams, and he knew a deadly serious situation had developed when he heard the burst of semi-automatic weapons fire and the "*Pop*" of an explosion forward. Unable to see exactly what was going on and unsure if he should take any action, he remained rooted to his seat as a man with a semi-automatic gun emerged from the mid galley onto the starboard aisle.

"I don't know how many there are, and I don't know who has weapons," thought Daniel. He reasoned it was better to remain where he was until he could figure things out, and prayed Tarkan was all right in his seat on the port side of coach.

The two remaining terrorists brandished their MP5K's in the faces of terrified passengers and began snapping plastic handcuffs on them. Resistance was futile in the face of the automatic weapons and loud threats in a strange language.

The *Irbis* team had no trouble acquiring everyone's passport, cell phone, and computer, and within ten minutes had bound everyone's hands with plastic ties.

Giorgi took the co-pilot's seat. Waving the Glock at the captain, he began barking commands in English. "Take it up to 35,000 and stay on a forty-two degree heading for Volgograd. Make no move on any of the instruments or controls without my approval. I've flown this type of aircraft before."

"Yes, yes. As you say. You don't need to point that at me," pleaded the captain.

Giorgi's knowledge of the cockpit and its blizzard of controls and dials amazed the Karaca captain. Giorgi motioned for the co-pilot to evacuate the cockpit, and as he was being led away, the man became agitated by the terrorists' manhandling. "You bastards!" he roared, trying to take a swing at Giorgi.

Enraged, Gustanov brought the full impact of his MP5K to the co-pilot's temple, yelling in Russian, "Shut up, asshole."

He followed this brutal assault with three more blows to the co-pilot's head, knocking him unconscious. The terrorists stuffed him into the baggage hold with the other crew members. All had their hands bound like the passengers, with a few blankets thrown on top of them after protests about potential hypothermia in the chilled cargo hold. The co-pilot eventually succumbed to his injuries.

Giorgi's men began patrolling the aisles, MP5Ks drawn, with safeties off.

The outside world, including Ataturk RATCC officials, was still unaware of the hijacking.

As his bound hands began to sweat, Daniel found his thoughts racing from his present situation to the things he cared about most: his struggling business and Arianna. Arianna?

He had to get out of this alive.

CHAPTER 7
Transformation - the Snow Leopard and the Ibex

KRA Flight 1025
At 35,000 feet over the Black Sea
August 10, 2008

Still on course for Volgograd, Giorgi continued to closely monitor the pilot's actions as KRA 1025 continued over the Black Sea. The dozens of hours of Giorgi's passenger-aircraft training in the Georgian military had paid off. He knew he could actually fly the plane himself if an adverse circumstance arose.

In the cabin Daniel took time to compose himself, realizing that these men would not risk a hijacking for an unimportant reason. Daniel had noted the aircraft's planned course on a map at Ataturk.

He also recalled the news bulletins of tensions building between Russia and Georgia, and thought, "Could the hijackers be terrorists from the Caucasus trying to exact damage on Russia because of a military conflict, similar to actions taken by Chechen separatists with bombings in Moscow?"

With a chill, Daniel pictured the worst possible scenario, "The hijackers might be using the aircraft and the passengers in it, including several Russian citizens, as a weapon just like the radical Islamists did on September 11, 2001!"

His memory of an previous encounter with an ibex merged with the more recent one from the Istanbul carpet shop: the snow leopard, enemy of the ibex, woven into the carpet. Predator and prey.

His mind relaxing, he let it drift, slowly, into a meditative state…

A sure-footed ibex gazed out over its realm of rocky crags, lichen-covered rocks, and small scrub junipers stunted by the harsh alpine environment. It searched for an easier but more dangerous route to a nearby cirque where grasses and moss outlined crevices among the rocks.

Unknown to the king of the Capricorn family, another visitor eyed its progress with anticipation. A rare snow leopard began to shadow the ibex's movements, planning its next meal! It was overcast and snowing lightly, conditions aiding the carnivore's camouflage.

The big cat stealthily approached the ibex, which was resting on a granite ledge. With his oversize paws muffling the sounds of his approach, the cat was able to get tantalizingly close before the ibex detected its presence and bounded up and away to a higher ledge. It changed direction a split-second later, using its sharp hooves with soft interior pads to their full friction-gripping advantage.

Back and forth the snow leopard chased the ibex across the jagged granite. The ibex's nimbleness allowed it to keep ahead of the large predator. The chase continued, but the ibex unknowingly headed into a steep section that limited its escape options. Then, a dead end!

The surrounding ledges were all vertical, impossible to scale. The snow leopard was just meters away, slowing as it sensed the end. There was no escape.

Except one possibility.

Just beyond the narrow ledge where it was trapped, the ibex saw the top of a small pillar of rock, separated from the ledge by two meters of open space. It was a sheer drop of ten meters on either side of the pillar. A fall from this point could result in injury or death for either animal.

The ibex paused ever so briefly, assessing its dangerous situation. Then it leapt onto the cylindrical pillar, barely one square meter in size and covered with hard snow over a thin layer of ice!

Its multi-tooled feet did not fail. Its sharp hooves penetrated the snow, allowing the soft pads inside its hooves to grab the ice and bits of granite underneath. The ibex landed steadily and confidently and whirled to face its predator.

The snow leopard paused, unsure of this opportunity. Its preferred terrain was the forests below, although it was capable of hunting on the higher rock. But it was hungry. It had been five days since its last meal. It was confident in its superior power. Any fall would be cushioned by its prey. It snarled and leapt!

Using all its instincts, when the cat was in midair, the ibex lowered its head, bringing its one meter curved horns to bear on the cat's face. Its hooves still firmly anchored in the ice and rock, it pushed forward with all its strength, smashing the cat with the scimitar-shaped weapons, throwing it off balance just enough to force its paws to splay wildly as it sought to regain equilibrium.

Too late!

Two of the cat's huge paws missed the rock pillar entirely and it fell from the precipice, still snarling.

Thud!

It landed on the rocks below. Bruised but otherwise unhurt.

Daniel was jolted from his meditative state. "The ibex knew its adversary's tactics, and knew how to use its horns to the best advantage," he thought. Now fully awake he recalled the most prominent elements of his dream.

"If only I had a weapon, anything to slow, or distract the terrorists," he said to himself. "I might as well die trying because everyone on board is likely to perish as pawns in the hijackers' sinister plans."

His mind was already in overdrive, dominated by memories, albeit painful ones, extracted from long ago, accompanied by solutions that flashed simultaneously into his consciousness. The military training he so despised as a teenager returned to guide him...

What is your primary objective?

"I must neutralize the terrorists advantage in weapons to re-take the aircraft. Because the terrorists are compartmentalized, if I gain one of their weapons and take out two of them, I can use the passengers to defeat the rest."

Know your enemy. Do a reconnaissance and evaluation of his position, his strengths and weaknesses.

"Best to classify the hijackers in an orderly fashion," Daniel reasoned. "That will make it easier to keep track of them. Since one of them is likely in the cockpit I'll call him #1 and work backward, left to right."

Wanting to get a better view of the others' locations, Daniel motioned to the nearest terrorist that he needed to use the toilet, The short, nervous-looking man in dark slacks and blue shirt was patrolling the rear starboard aisle. Keeping his MP5K in his right hand he escorted Daniel, hands still bound in front of him, to the starboard first class lav, as all other lavatories were made off limits so they could easily control access to one lav. As the terrorist shoved him up the aisle, Daniel passed another hijacker who was guarding the mid-starboard section, wearing a black athletic jacket with white stripes on the sleeves.

Glancing around the cabin as he trudged forward Daniel noted, "Looks like each of these two men on the starboard side has a counterpart on the port aisle. That's four men."

Another terrorist, whom the others called "Gustanov," an evil-looking man with a ruddy complexion, patrolled both sides of the first class cabin and the lav where Daniel was headed.

Gustanov sought to gain respect by being curt, rude, and ruthless to both the passengers and his comrades. And when he came upon a row of passengers speaking Russian in low tones he grew enraged.

"Silence. No talking," he yelled in Russian. When one female passenger showed the slightest indignation at being treated rudely, Gustanov pistol-whipped her into submission with two blows from the MP5K in his right hand. When a male passenger tried to get up to protect her, Gustanov smashed him across the face, then the back of the head with the weapon. Both passengers bled from facial and head wounds but received no treatment.

During his walk back from the forward lavatory Daniel heard another name, "Datshi," who was in the mid galley and periodically walked the length of the mid portside aisle, occasionally eyeballing an attractive woman in his section.

The nervous-looking hijacker returned Daniel to his seat, 34F, and resumed his beat in the aft section of the starboard side.

Daniel summarized his recon exercize: "That makes five out here and the leader in the cockpit, six altogether. #2, Gustanov, guarding first class; #3, Datshi, mid-portside aisle; #4 with the black athletic jacket patrolling the mid-starboard aisle; #5 in the aft portside section; and #6, closest to me in the aft-starboard position."

Having placed the positions of all six terrorists, Daniel began to plan a way out of his imprisoned position with his newly-discovered source of power—his past.

CHAPTER 8
Counterstrike!

KRA Flight 1025.
At 35,000 feet over the Black Sea, 400 kilometers east of
Sevastopol, Crimea, Ukraine.
August 10, 2008

Develop a battle plan, an immediate scope of engagement.
Daniel burned into his memory the next three steps he
must achieve in rapid succession: gain one of the terrorist's
weapons, take out the cabin terrorists with the help of
passengers, and disarm the lead terrorist in the cockpit.
That done, he would have to hope someone was left to fly
the airplane!

Daniel's seat on the starboard aft aisle was ideal, as he
had only two adversaries to immediately worry about, #4
and #6. But he had to time his action for when terrorists
Datshi, Gustanov, who were forward, and #5, were at the
farthest part of their beats. Daniel estimated this would give
him three to four seconds to disable #6, acquire his weapon
and take out #4 and #5 before #5 could secure a hostage as
a shield. A calculated risk that appeared unavoidable.

If he was to surprise the #6 terrorist he would need to use a backward movement with his right arm. But all of this planning would be useless if he could not free his hands from the plastic handcuffs. For several minutes he stared straight ahead, his mind searching for a solution.

You must have weapons. You may have to improvise.

Out of the corner of his eye he saw his immediate neighbor, an elderly but spritely looking woman, motion with her eyes downward. Daniel glanced and—lo!—saw two white plastic objects concealed beneath her hands. A plastic knife and fork! Discovered in her magazine pouch, no doubt.

The white curves of the plastic ware reminded him of something. *"The horns of the ibex!"* Daniel exclaimed softly.

The terrorists seemed to hold all the cards. But Daniel's dream had given him a new outlook, a higher awareness, an ability to use shrewdness and daring, even in high risk situations.

Use the enemy's own tactics against him.

Take them on at their own game. *Terror!* And with the gift from the elderly lady next to him, Daniel realized he had the tools to take the fight to the hijackers. He took the two plastic utensils and stuffed them into the crevice next to his left seat arm, nodding quickly to the older woman, acknowledging her precious gift.

Flight 1025 was approaching the Russian coast and Giorgi's excitement grew with every minute. He allowed himself time for a reflection: "Yes, Father and Mother," he thought, "I am avenging your deaths now. I am with you, just like the magical moments when Father and I hunted together."

"Soon we will approach land," said the captain, snapping Giorgi out of his reflection. The terrorist leader recognized he must make a painful decision. It was time to dispose of the captain. No sense in keeping alive a potential threat, one who might also alert the Russian air traffic controllers.

He rose from the co-pilot's seat and said to the captain, "You have done well so far. Thank you for being cooperative. You have fared better than your co-pilot who chose his actions poorly," as he moved to stretch just out of the officer's view.

"You are welcome. No sense making foolish moves ..." As the captain completed his sentence Giorgi turned away from him while pulling an assault knife from his jacket pocket. Quickly, he dispatched the captain by slicing his neck from behind and watched him bleed to death.

Terrorist #6 slowly walked his starboard beat aft, passing Daniel on his right. Daniel had been carefully counting the number of steps the man took from his seat at 34F, to reach the end of his walk. Daniel began to saw the plastic cuffs with the serated plastic knife while the hijacker was farthest away.

Over the course of the terrorist's next three beats, Daniel managed to sever the cuffs, freeing both his hands, replacing the knife and fork between his legs to escape detection.

When facing a force of superior strength, Strike first! Strike fast! Strike hard!

As he freed himself, he recalled the words of his high school football coach who told the team as they were about to take the field against a much bigger opponent: "Remember—when up against overwhelming odds, there is always a solution to everything. Do something they least suspect!"

He took the plastic knife in his right hand, with the blade pointed backward. The fork was in his left hand, positioned for a forward stabbing motion.

This was it.

As the man passed to go aft, Daniel began the count: twelve steps. That took him to the end of the beat. Then he commenced twelve steps forward.

Four, five, six, seven…Wait. The man stopped!

Daniel dared not look back to find the cause. After an excruciating pause, the man resumed his walk forward.

Eight, Nine, Ten.

Daniel unbuckled his seat belt and edged slightly off the seat, his feet planted firmly.

He would need to gain as much leverage as possible to inflict the maximum damage.

Eleven, twelve!

Now!

In a lightning fast move, Daniel swung his right arm backward, his fist at the same level as the terrorist's crotch jamming the plastic knife into the man's groin with all his strength. With a precision gained as if he had been practicing this move all his life, Daniel wheeled his left foot into the aisle directly in front of the man. In a split second, the terrorist doubled over to protect himself.

Anticipating this, Daniel's left hand was already in motion while springing from his left foot, with the plastic fork positioned for his second blow, unopposed by the surprised terrorist whose hands had gone to protect his groin.

But Daniel's next strike did not require speed or power, as much as accuracy. Grasping the fork tightly in his left fist, tines pointed forward, he stabbed toward another vital body part. The man's right eye!

A hideous scream confirmed the accuracy of Daniel's aim, as three tines of the plastic tool penetrated all the way into the man's optic nerve, severing the ophthalmic artery and shredding several arteries surrounding the eye, drawing copious flows of blood and hysterical cries from his victim. To elicit maximum effect, Daniel twisted the fork counterclockwise, still maintaining forward pressure, severing the rest of the arteries and ripping the eye partially out of its socket.

With the terrorist incapacitated, Daniel thrust off his right foot and extended his right hand toward the next objective, the black grip and trigger of the MP5K slung over the man's right shoulder. In the same motion, he twisted the weapon inward toward the terrorist's heart and left lung while squeezing the trigger. A one-second burst instantly terminated the man's life. Several passengers screamed in fright at the sound of the violence.

With the first terrorist dispatched and bleeding profusely on the aisle carpet, Daniel yanked the weapon away from him and wheeled 180 degrees to aim at what he guessed would be his next target, the #4 terrorist coming to investigate the sound of gunshots and his comrade's screams. Flattening himself behind the slain man's body, Daniel hunkered down as #4 sprinted toward him, MP5K raised, the trigger set for single-shot.

The terrorist fired first, a wild shot, his aim affected by surprise and his running movements. The round glanced off an overhead compartment and embedded itself harmlessly in a rear bulkhead. He took a second, more accurate shot that would have hit Daniel, were it not for the protective barrier of the dead terrorist, whose torso stopped the bullet. But now Daniel was ready to take an accurate shot from his own MP5K.

Aiming for the man's chest, Daniel fired twice hitting #4's torso and his legs. The man's knees collapsed and he fell face forward, gushing blood and unable to return fire.

Daniel quickly relieved #6 of his Glock 7, assault knife, and spare rounds.

Use all available resources. Ask for help.

Terrorist #5, on the aft port aisle, was blinded to the action by the rows of passengers between him and Daniel. The sound of gunfire caused him to temporarily retreat to the center galley and Datshi drew back to the first class galley where Gustanov was also huddled. Realizing that passengers might be at risk of being used as human shields by #5, Daniel quickly fashioned another strategy. In a low voice, he asked the passengers within earshot, "Anyone know how to use a gun?"

"I do," came a reply from the middle starboard section.

Daniel moved quickly to the man's position. "Hold out your hands," he commanded. The man obeyed and Daniel sliced the man's plastic handcuffs with a single motion of the assault knife. "What's your name?" he asked.

"Bill Casey. Canadian Coast Guard Reserve."

"Thank God. Somebody who knows how to use these things," Daniel said.

"Take these," Daniel said as he tossed the man a Glock 17 and spare clips. "You go down this aisle. There's a terrorist in the center section on the port aisle who may try to take a hostage. If he does, I will distract him. He doesn't know you're in this aisle and he doesn't know you are armed. When he gets set to shoot me you take him out. Do your best to avoid hitting any hostages, but the number one priority is to kill the terrorist. You may have only one shot. Make it count! *Kill him* or we're all going down."

He handed the knife to another passenger after cutting his plastic cuffs, "Free all the passengers. Now!" Then he nodded toward Bill.

As Bill moved forward down the starboard aisle, keeping his body low, Daniel raced forward, keeping his eyes alert for terrorist #5. Sure enough, as Bill passed row 23, he saw the man grab a female passenger in 22D in an attempt to shield himself.

Meanwhile, Daniel leapfrogged the center section seats and landed on the port aisle. Taking aim at the terrorist, he fired a single shot with his MP5K. But with his target partially obscured, the round penetrated a seat cushion on the opposite side of the aisle with a soft *Pfftt!* Terrorist #5 crouched behind the passenger as he struggled to undo her seat belt. Daniel still didn't have a clear shot.

However, before Daniel crossed to the port side of the aircraft, he failed to ensure the status of terrorist #4 on the starboard side. Crumpled up on top of his weapon, the man was severely wounded but not dead. Slowly he stirred. Grimacing with pain, he was able to get to his knees, his shaking hands slowly bringing his MPK5 around and up to bear on Bill's exposed back as the Canadian Coast Guard

Reserve officer edged forward in a crouch. Terrorist #4 gasped, "Got him in my sights…just another second…"

BAM!

#4 reeled from an unseen blow. Then another, and another. Forced to the floor, the weapon fell from his trembling hands. "What the…?" he thought. How…?"

BAM!

Another blow to the wound in his left ribs. Relentless pain. Too late, he realized his fate was sealed.

"It's the passengers! They are going to kill me!" #4 screamed. He begged for mercy. One passenger actually laughed as he wrested the MP5K from under the man's body.

"*Mudak!*" Asshole! The passenger hissed. "You want mercy when you have been trying to kill us! You are a dead man!" He took the assault knife being passed around by the passengers and, with a sweeping motion from left to right, severed the man's carotid arteries and larynx. Full of adrenaline after facing an almost certain death, the passenger raised the assault knife a meter above the terrorist's head and plunged the weapon into the man's face, penetrating all the way through his skull, pinning the terrorist's head to the floor of the aircraft.

The surrounding passengers cheered and pulled every component of combat gear from the dead man's body. The bloodied assault knife continued its journey from passenger to passenger as they sliced themselves free of their plastic bonds. Daniel heard, then saw, the disturbance on the starboard side. He understood #4 was dead for sure, but more importantly, that the passengers were now engaged in resistance! And they were energized. They could now be allies in taking the fight to the terrorists.

Daniel glanced over at the portside rows where Tarkan was sitting. He appeared to be okay and was having his plastic handcuffs cut just as Daniel caught sight of him, "I'll have to catch up with him later," he thought.

But #5 was still a threat. The terrorist successfully wrestled the female passenger to her feet and, crouching behind her, began to advance aft down the port aisle toward Daniel's position, holding his MP5K to the hostage's head.

When Daniel saw the terrorist's protective position and realized he could not hit him, he raised his hands and dropped his weapon. Hijacker #5 continued to advance, bringing his MP5K to bear on Daniel's body, he smirked in Russian, "Hah. You American? Only Americans try such stupid things. You John Wayne? Hah. You are dead pig!"

His grip on his hostage relaxed, so he could take better aim at Daniel.

The man's cruel ranting was his undoing as it allowed Bill to track his movements through the openings along the seat rows. The Canadian officer rose above the level of the passengers' heads in mid section, his Glock 17 pointed at the hijacker. When he saw the woman released, Bill knew the time to shoot was now.

Just before terrorist #5 could fire, he sensed movement and an unanticipated danger to his left. Turning to get a better look…

Pop! Pop! Bill squeezed off two shots in quick succession. The first, aimed at the man's torso which offered a more exposed position; the second directed at the man's head.

Both rounds found their mark, blood spattering nearby passengers and seat cushions. The head shot exited the man's skull and lodged in the fiberglass cover of an overhead bin, causing passengers in that row to scream and duck down in their seats.

Daniel raced forward to the mid galley. "Good shooting, Bill. That's three down, three to go! Two more must have run forward. I'll meet you in the midway galley."

"Roger," yelled Bill.

Cowed by their comrades' failures, Gustanov and Datshi remained hunkered down in the first class galley. In their haste they forgot about trying to harm the first class passengers. Gustanov, ducked behind food prep equipment in the port side and Datshi retreated to the starboard side of the galley.

A quantum shift had occurred inside the aircraft. Previously the terrorists were the sole masters of power, their quarry bound helpless, with no way to strike at their evil captors. But after Daniel's lightning counterstrike, it was the terrorists facing a condition previously unknown to them: The fear that comes from facing someone determined to terminate their lives.

The passengers, emboldened and empowered, advanced to stalk their new-found prey, carrying the weapons of the three dispatched hijackers. They did so carefully, ducking in and out of the rows of seats, still aware the terrorists had automatic weapons.

At this point Gustanov and Datshi saw each other, and Gustanov called frantically to Giorgi for directions.

Beware of overconfidence.

Daniel paused. In a flash he had grown out of his mild-mannered shell and pursued the high risk game of hunting—other humans. A totally new sensation. Like a drug injected into his veins had kicked in and drove him to his next encounter.

"Better slow down a bit," he thought. "If I get hasty, these evil men will defeat me. They are far more experienced with these weapons than I. I'll need help, and now is not the time to get cocky."

He knew dispatching the remaining terrorists would require creativity, as he had now lost the element of surprise. This was not going to be a Lone Ranger shoot-out. The terrorists still had numerical superiority and could shield themselves behind other passengers, complicating his task immensely. He had to be careful but act quickly.

Daniel shouted to the nearby passengers, "Anyone else know how to use a gun?

"Folks, the hijackers are probably going to crash the plane into some ground objective they want to destroy," he addressed them. "Our only chance is to defeat them now. Otherwise we're all gonna die."

Even though the passengers were still terrified, one man spoke up. "I know how to use a gun." Daniel tossed him one of the Glock pistols and three extra clips. "Great. What's your name?"

"Matt Carpenter. I was with the LAPD for twelve years. Be glad to help out."

Daniel, Matt and Bill huddled for a few moments. They relied on passengers' observations that the two terrorists had taken refuge in the first class galley.

"If we can take them with knives it will reduce the chance of a passenger being hit by a bullet and lower the chance of gunfire piercing a window, which will blow cabin pressure," Matt advised. "We should keep the Glocks handy in case we can't close the distance to engage them with our knives." Daniel took one of the assault knives after the passengers had freed their hands.

Bill nodded. "MP5Ks around our necks ready to shoot, Glocks and knives in our pockets. Safeties off," said Bill.

"They will be watching the aisles," Daniel pointed out to Matt. "If we 'boogie step' over the seatbacks in the far left and right mid sections they might not see us. Once we're opposite their estimated positions we can fire a couple of rounds with the Glocks through the thin partitions which might smoke them out to where we can use the knives at close quarters."

Nodding in agreement again, Daniel and Matt alternately leapt and scrambled over left section and right section cabin seats until they were one row removed from the first class galley.

As Daniel and Matt advanced, Bill crept slowly down the starboard aisle, MP5K at the ready, with a Glock in his right jacket pocket and assault knife in the left to support the proposed attack by the other two. He was to act in reserve while Daniel and Matt initiated the battle on the terrorists in first class.

Daniel and Matt crouched behind first class Row 1, its passengers already having moved aft, away from immediate danger. But Daniel hesitated. What if the hijackers were waiting for them?

Do what your enemy would least suspect.

Relying on cunning and instinct, Daniel created a new strategy on the fly. Glancing at the row of two first class seats behind him, seats 2A and 2B, he noticed an intelligent-looking man of about forty-five and a twelve or thirteen year-old boy who appeared to be his son.

Daniel squeezed into the space in front of the boy and began to speak in a low voice to both passengers, keeping his glance mainly directed at the man. "We are facing ruthless terrorists who will stop at nothing until we're all dead.

"I'm prepared to continue the fight but I need a little insurance. Something they won't suspect should the they gain the upper hand in the next encounter. They won't be anticipating weapons fire from your boy, here." The man nodded his understanding but was clearly rattled.

Daniel looked at the boy and asked his name.

"Bobby Andrews," was his reply.

His father realized this plan might be their last hope and nodded.

Daniel handed the boy the Glock and advised "Bobby, you hold it like this, keep the safety off with this, remember, it's a live weapon now. Squeeze the trigger to fire, just like you've seen in movies and on TV. You look like you have strong hands. Use both of them to hold the weapon. And fire only when I give the okay."

Meanwhile Giorgi called out to his men, frantically asking what was going on. Gustanov replied, "A passenger has broken free and killed three of our men with their own weapons; we are holed up in the first class galley."

"Kill them!" Giorgi yelled. "I am flying the plane and must remain in the cockpit. Keep silent lest they discover your exact positions and mount an attack on you.

Daniel and Matt signaled each other that now was the time to execute their plan.

They fired a burst with their submachine pistols, directing their shots through the partitions encasing port and starboard sections of the first class galley. Their target was the last-known location of the hijackers provided by nearby passengers. They speculated the submachine bursts would also temporarily disorient the hijackers, giving them a second or so advantage.

Create a reserve position to facilitate retreat or protect gains made on the battlefield.

Daniel had re-positioned Bill in row fifteen, in a reserve position, to protect the bulk of the passengers in case the terrorists gained the advantage during the firefight. Both Daniel who was on the left and Matt on the right, had a sweeping view of the first class galleys and lavatory sections. Daniel nodded and they opened fire again with their MP5Ks in two short bursts. They paused.

Silence.

Now they had to take a big risk. Since the terrorists did not flush out during the gunfire Daniel and Matt had to force their hand. Together they dived toward the two openings in the first class galley, twisting sideways so they could fire again. But Gustanov stayed protected behind the galley's stainless steel infrastructure and Datshi was still safe in his position.

With his feet balanced on the galley prep surfaces, Gustanov fired downward in three-second bursts at Daniel and Matt, vulnerable on the galley floor. Quickly Daniel realized their predicament and, with bullets whizzing overhead, attempted to retreat to the safety of the port lavatory. But he was too slow moving backward. The last half burst from Gustanov caught him in the left arm, one bullet hitting him in the tricep, another grazing his forearm, before he managed to stagger back into the port side lav.

In the shootout he lost his grip on the MP5K and it fell harmlessly to the floor, where Gustanov was able to retrieve it. Back in the protection of the lav, Daniel used the lower portion of his left sleeve to bind his tricep wound, then ripped his right sleeve halfway up and made a temporary bandage for his forearm, slowing the bleeding in both wounds.

Matt was less fortunate. Datshi, being taller, had a better angle and pressed his height advantage above Matt, pumping a full one-second burst into his buttocks and right leg. Yelling in pain and bleeding profusely, Matt made a superhuman effort to crawl away. In his pain he lost his grip on the MP5K, which fell to the galley floor. He pulled himself with his arms around the galley section and tumbled into the starboard lav, closing the fiberglass door behind him.

Now both Daniel and Matt were wounded, vulnerable, and trapped in the forward lavs. Matt suffered the worst wounds, temporarily losing his ability to walk, and both men had lost their semi-automatic weapons. Matt still had his Glock, but all Daniel had was an assault knife in his right rear pocket. Bill was still in reserve, protecting the passengers, and did not have a clean shot at the terrorists.

Datshi leapt down from his galley perch and grabbed Matt's discarded MP5K, grinning confidently and shouting the results of the last encounter to Giorgi. "Yes," yelled Giorgi, pumping his fist in triumph. But then he screamed at his men to finish off their victims, "We are on the verge of victory. Kill these pigs now! And don't damage the plane."

Hearing this order from his leader, Gustanov jumped in front of the port side first class lav and opened fire with two bursts through the thin fiberglass door.

But his angle of fire assumed Daniel was standing upright inside the lav. Confident he had dispatched his prey, Gustanov kicked at the flimsy door, fully expecting to find his adversary dead on the floor. But Daniel had wedged himself in the upper reaches of the lav. As the door burst open, he leapt feet-first toward the opening, hoping to catch the terrorist off guard. His body flew out but only caught the terrorist a with glancing blow.

Gustanov was forced back only two steps and laughed cruelly to see his enemy helpless on the floor before him. Datshi had advanced to the starboard side of the aircraft with the intention of finishing off Matt.

Daniel struggled to regain his feet, knowing his adversary was right above him on the port aisle. But as he got to one knee, Gustanov kicked him in the head, sending him reeling backward against the floor, then knocked him to the floor again with his left fist. With a mocking laugh, Gustanov aimed his MP5K at Daniel for one final burst, "Hah, your are American? You die by my hand you pig."

But Daniel gave a defiant, desperate yell. "*Shoot, Bobby!*"

A confused look of fear grew on the terrorist's face. Was there a vulnerability he hadn't anticipated? Did the Western pig have an ally? He began a half turn to look aft when:

BAM! BAM!

Bobby pulled the trigger on the Glock twice. The first round missed wildly, hitting the forward galley bulkhead, the weapon almost recoiling out of his untrained hand. But his second shot struck Gustanov in the right shoulder, spinning him counterclockwise and forcing him on his back on the galley prep surface.

But Gustanov still clutched his semiautomatic machine pistol. If he could just rock to a sitting position he could surely deal with this new threat…

Distracted by the slug in his shoulder, Gustanov missed seeing Daniel roll to the floor as he moved out of the terrorist's line of sight. The American advanced two steps toward the galley prep area in a crouched position. His uninjured arm pulled out the last weapon of defense, the twelve-inch-long assault knife. "I must strike quickly," thought Daniel. "I don't think he saw me move closer. I may have only two seconds to make my next move …"

Daniel's transformation from a meek businessman to an aggressive fighter was complete. He had turned into a killing machine. He had assimilated the terrorist mentality, where fear and ruthlessness took over the mild, courteous manner of his former self.

The shock of potentially losing his business, missing the chance to express his love to Arianna, and the desire to build the institutions and spirits of others had been pushed aside by the need for victory in combat. His aggressive, military shadow self that had been repressed as a teenager had fully returned.

Gustanov regained his balance and rocked forward, yelling in Russian, "I will get you now!" He swung his MP5K around to get a bead on Daniel's position on the floor, still not seeing him, who was now crouched just below the terrorist, waiting for the right moment to strike.

Daniel waited for the first unprotected body part of his adversary that presented itself, the soft underside of his jaw. With a newfound cruelty of his own, Daniel swung the assault knife with a vicious upward thrust, grinding his knife through the tongue, the soft palate, the nasal cavity, and into the lower part of Gustanov's brain. The terrorist, stupefied by the deadly blow, ceased all motion, his tongue now pinned in a fixed position within his mouth.

He tried to speak but could only utter a small moan, as if to convey his bewilderment at the turn of events. But he could still move the MP5K in his right arm, and he slowly moved it into firing position.

Daniel, his peripheral vision on overdrive, was aware of the terrorist's final act of desperation.

With his right arm holding Gustanov's head on the knife like a stuck pig, Daniel hesitated a split second, gazing into the terrorist's eyes with a combined look of revenge and total disregard for the man's life. Then he let out a yell and used his wounded left arm to bat away Gustanov's weapon, which fell harmlessly on the galley surface.

Daniel exhaled another shout of pain as he swung his left arm to a double grip on the knife. Cruelly, he twisted it in a clockwise, upward motion, doubling the size of the wound, as the tip of the knife acted like a corkscrew penetrating deeper into the man's lower frontal lobe. Gustanov screamed, muffled by his tongue which was pinned to the roof of his mouth. Then came a whimper, almost as if for mercy. He died seconds later, frozen in a semi-seated position, blood pouring from his lower jaw, mouth, and nasal cavity. Daniel seized Gustanov's assault knife and sliced the terrorist's neck, severing the man's right carotid artery and leaving both knives embedded in the terrorist's body. Blood gushed forth, turning the man's clothes crimson.

Even as he set Gustanov's butchered body in a rigid position on the galley, Daniel had already planned his next moves against Datshi.

Giorgi was desperate to find out what happened and yelled for his men. Datshi gave him a hurried response. They had wounded two passengers in a shoot out, adding that he could no longer see Gustanov. "Find him," Giorgi screamed, "and stick together."

Giorgi noted the aircraft was nearing the Russian coast at Anapa. Hopefully no one had noticed their hijacking activities.

But someone had.

A controller in the Ataturk RACC spotted a blinking signal just below the symbol for KRA 1025 on his screen. The yellow flash indicated that the aircraft had not issued its routine check-in code, a practice all captains of commercial flights were required to perform. He alerted his supervisor immediately.

Anticipate what your adversary will do. Then create countermeasures.

Daniel now clearly saw a strategy to dispatch terrorist Datshi, but first he had to lure him closer. He poked his head from behind the central galley fixture just enough for Datshi to respond with a burst from his semi-automatic, the rounds penetrating a panel in the galley. Daniel retreated behind the galley, counting to five, his estimate of the time it would take Datshi to arrive at the opposite side of the same galley fixture.

Distracted by the swift chain of events, Datshi bolted a few meters aft and hurriedly fired at the starboard lav, where Matt still lay critically wounded.

Too hurriedly. The rounds penetrated the fiberglass lav door but passed harmlessly over Matt's head. Confident he had hit his adversary but not being able to see inside the lav, Datshi surmised he could finish the job later.

He approached the starboard side of the first class galley, his weapon covering the place where he last saw Daniel. Cautiously sneaking around to the front of the food prep station, Datshi saw a pair of legs and feet protruding from the upper part of the galley. He couldn't tell who it was but recalled that Daniel was wearing jeans. This must be his adversary! Datshi was jubilant to discover his prey in sight with no opposing weapon confronting him. He fired off another burst at the dangling legs, making them jerk violently.

"This is too easy," he thought, changing his magazine before he sprinted in front of the galley to finish off his target with another burst. He could already see large quantities of blood sputtering from the thighs, knees and calves of his helpless adversary.

As Datshi raised his MP5K to deliver the coup de grâce, he stopped dead in his tracks, a look of sheer horror in his eyes and his face contorted with fear. Above the bleeding legs he thought belonged to Daniel was a sight his eyes could not bear to behold, yet the horror was so extreme he could not shift his eyes away.

Staring straight at him was the bloody head of Gustanov, an assault knife buried in his skull from the soft part of his lower jaw, a gaping wound surrounding the knife's entry. A second knife extended from a semi-circular slice across the neck, from which blood continued to cascade down the front of the body to the top of the galley.

"Gustanov! He is dead! He must have…but how…?" The terrorist's mind raced. "If Gustanov was here, dead, that meant his adversary was somewhere nearby and must be stopped!" Datshi spun to take evasive action—

Too late.

There, confronting him head-on, was Daniel, pointing Gustanov's MP5K directly at his face, only inches away. Though he was wounded, Daniel had been able to mirror the terrorist's movements on the opposite side of the galley, creeping clockwise along the port side while the terrorist moved counterclockwise around the starboard side. When he heard the Datshi's clumsy actions, shooting at an unidentified set of legs, Daniel guessed Datshi was going in for the kill and quickly closed the distance.

With thoughts of amazement and fear running through his head, Datshi raised his weapon in a last-ditch effort to escape death and managed to squeeze off another one-second burst. But without time to aim the weapon, the rounds bounced harmlessly off the floor of the aircraft.

At the same instant, Daniel pulled the trigger on his machine pistol. ***Thud, thud, thud, thud, thud.*** Five rounds split Datshi's face and skull, entering his brain, killing him instantly.

He asked two passengers on the starboard side to check for visible damage to the exterior, "Have you noticed anything that might have damaged the hull of the aircraft?"

At first he only received bewildered looks. "Oh, sorry. *Gavaruh Engleski?*" Daniel tried again in very primitive Russian. Over the next few minutes a translator was able to help him determine that no one had noticed any damage to either side of the aircraft's exterior.

Giorgi was yelling madly through the open cockpit door for a status update. He realized too late that the door could not be latched or locked as the terrorists themselves blew open the lock with C4 earlier in the flight. He called three times for the two men he believed remained, his voice rising in desperation.

Daniel thought quickly. "It seems like the only language these bastards understand is terror. Well, that's what we used on all of his men. Let's see if it works on their leader."

CHAPTER 9
All the Marbles

KRA Flight 1025.
At 35,000 feet over the Black Sea, 100 kilometers south of the
Russian coast at Anapa
August 10, 2008

Daniel approached Bobby and his father. "Thank you,
Bobby," patting his shoulder. "You saved my life. I'll speak
with you and your father later."

Suspecting Matt was critically wounded, Daniel turned
to Bill to explain a new strategy. Bill was uninjured and
appeared in excellent physical shape.

Daniel asked the nearest passengers, "Please look after
our friend. He is wounded in the starboard lavatory. Hurry!"
Two passengers in first class responded immediately. Finding
Matt in the starboard lav, they took him back down the aisle
to a safer locale. Someone shouted for a doctor.

Daniel turned to three more passengers and said
urgently, "Please release the crew from the hold. There is an
access trap door in the center of first class. If you can't open
it, use a shot from this Glock pistol to dislodge the latch," as

he handed them the weapon previously used by Bobby. The passengers immediately rushed aft to comply.

Strike while your enemy is distracted.

Daniel briefly explained his plan to Bill, stressing the importance of keeping the cockpit door jammed open.

Giorgi cracked the cockpit door to check in with his men. He yelled for them to speak, but when there was no answer in Georgian he attempted to close the door. But both Daniel and Bill were ready. They kept their MP5Ks trained on the open cockpit door.

Daniel fired two single shots that forced Giorgi back to the captain's seat. "Look at the blood!" Bill gasped. "He must have offed the captain."

"The co-pilot and pilot are both dead," said Daniel. "Only the lead terrorist knew how to fly the airplane. "He must have stuffed the captain's body in the co-pilot's seat so as not to arouse suspicion among the passengers or even his own men."

"Yeah, and when we dispatch the terrorist who's gonna fly the plane?" asked Bill.

Suddenly, a loud squawking emanated from the cockpit, and they heard Giorgi attempting to reply to a radio transmission and began a descent to lower altitude, 12,000 feet, to make it appear on radar like something had happened to the plane.

"The terrorist leader must have not known about some requirement that perhaps only the captain would have known," Daniel thought.

He motioned to Bill to grab Gustanov's body. Bill dragged the dead terrorist directly in front of the cockpit while Daniel kept his MP5K trained on the door to prevent the lead terrorist from closing it.

But Giorgi was now facing new problems.

Another radio message. Giorgi realized he must stall for time. "1025, Roger," he responded.

After a few moments Ataturk RATCC grew suspicious. "1025, acknowledge you are under normal flight conditions."

"KRA 1025, Roger. We have had heavy turbulence and a lightning strike. We have thirty-six Russian citizens aboard, along with 150 other passengers. Request emergency landing sequence in Volgograd."

This was the first notification to the outside world that something was wrong. Giorgi checked again, confirming the aircraft's course would take it directly over the Lukoil refinery and the desired spot of maximum impact. He locked it in to the software thumb drive so that no one could make changes to the plane's course without entering the proper code into the airplane's navigation computer.

The radio broke in again. "1025 This is Ataturk RATCC. Why are you at 12,000 feet altitude?"

"Emergency decompression," Giorgi responded. "Loss of cabin pressure, due to lightning strike. Descended to 12,000 feet to reduce further risk to passengers."

"KRA 1025, code in ID," demanded the Ataturk RATCC operator.

At this request, Giorgi switched off all radios. He knew it was useless to deceive the RATCC any further. He increased the airliner's speed to its maximum of 490 knots, knowing he only had a short time before other authorities were notified. The aircraft was now burning fuel at a rate of 220 pounds per minute. Giorgi glanced at the fuel gauge to assure himself there would be enough to reach Volgograd and still cause a significant fireball on impact.

To his horror, he discovered only 14,000 pounds of fuel remained—only just enough to get to Volgograd, far less than he expected!

"What could be causing the excess fuel loss?" he wondered, devastated at the discovery there wouldn't be much fuel left to cause a massive explosion at the refinery.

Unknown to him, the onboard firefight had produced a casualty even more damaging than the loss of his *Irbis* team. A stray bullet had penetrated the electronic switching center of the plane's avionics system, shorting out a relay that operated the aircraft's emergency fuel dumping valves, dispersing copious quantities of fuel for over an hour.

His original objective now seemed impossible!

"But wait!. I still have a chance!" reasoned Giorgi. "Nikolai was arranging for an extra 120,000 cubic meters of natural gas to be stored at the strike point. That alone should be enough for widespread damage!"

The aircraft continued its north-by-northeast course. Giorgi called to his men again. No answer. Cursing, he realized something had gone terribly wrong in the cabin and he had to stop losing fuel. He turned to make a desperate attempt to lock the cockpit door when…

BAM!

Daniel and Bill heaved Gustanov's body through the cockpit door, partially blocking the opening. The two knives in the terrorist's skull and neck were still in place. Giorgi saw the condition of his fellow terrorist and for a split-second was frozen by horror. Daniel followed up immediately by storming the cockpit in a horizontal leap, his Glock ready.

In that crucial second, before Giorgi could gain his composure, Daniel fired two single-shots before crashing into the forward control panel, the first striking the terrorist in the left lung, the second in the center of the chest. Blood erupted from both wounds. Giorgi slumped back in the co-pilot's seat, his lifeblood draining. His slowing mind grasped one final thought, "Father, Mother, I have done my best to avenge your deaths…"

All the terrorists were dead!

The RATCC operator at Ataturk was now convinced something was terribly wrong and immediately pressed a button on his console, alerting his shift supervisor. He then radioed authorities in Sevastopol, Ukraine, and Novorossiysk, Russia, and relayed the chain of events in English.

Daniel grabbed the body of the terrorist and began to haul it out of the pilot's chair but was impeded by the injury to his left arm. Bill noticed his difficulty and assisted in dragging the body out of the cockpit into the first class galley area.

"Bill, see if you can get some of the passengers to stow the body. And the captain may be in the small closet next to the cockpit. See if you can get him out. I've got to radio for help flying the plane. Ask any of the passengers if anyone has any flight experience. Anything will be a help maneuvering this baby. And then get back here. I may need your help some more! Thanks, man."

Then Daniel jumped into the bloodied captain's seat and tried a couple of knobs, until he discovered the radio comm link. "Now if I only knew how to work this thing…"

Squawk…! A voice coming over the comm link startled him. "Is this still KRA 1025?"

"Yes, this is KRA 1025. Who is this?" Daniel inquired.

"My name is Evren Bastyr. I am the regional air traffic controller at Ataturk RATCC. Please explain your situation."

Daniel complied, "I'm Daniel Prescott, a passenger onboard the Karaca Airlines 1025 airplane. Just after takeoff from Ataturk we were hijacked by armed terrorists, I think Georgian and Chechen. The captain and co-pilot are dead but all 181 passengers are unharmed. I was assisted by other passengers in eliminating the six terrorists."

There were a few moments of silence before Bastyr responded, "You mean the six terrorists are dead now?"

"Yes"

"Who is flying the aircraft?"

"Uhh, its on automatic pilot."

"There is no one flying the plane?"

Just then, Bill returned to the cockpit, shaking his head, "No luck. No one knows how to fly"

"No. I'm afraid you're going to have to advise me how to fly this thing," said Daniel to Bastyr.

"I can do that, but there is another controller in a better position to assist you, and he is directly connected with the Russian military should any emergencies arise," responded Bastyr.

The Ataturk RATCC transferred Daniel to the head air traffic control officer at Novorossiysk, Russia.

Novorossiysk Military Air Base
Novorossiysk, Russia
August 10, 2008

Lt. Commander Uri Krassnyansk was the chief air traffic controller on duty at the Novorossiysk Military Airfield, and was listening to commercial airliner chatter as a normal part of his duties.

Krassnyansk, an experienced fighter and airline pilot himself, received the radio transfer from Ataturk. He pulled up the flight on his screen and recognized something might be wrong with KRA 1025 due to its low altitude. He then raised Bastyr at the RATCC at Ataturk and demanded an explanation. In a minute he was satisfied he had enough data to engage in emergency procedures.

"This is Commander Krassnyansk of the Russian Air Force," he addressed Flight 1025. "Who am I speaking with?"

Daniel repeated his story to Krassnyansk.

Although startled at the news, Krassnyansk remained calm, true to his military training. "First tell me the status of your key instruments," he said, and he guided Daniel to the proper gauges showing the aircraft's vital signs.

Daniel repeated what he read on the dials: "Altimeter - 12,000 feet, Airspeed - 490 knots, Fuel - 7,560."

"Hmm," said Krassnyansk. "Did you say fuel was 7,560 pounds?"

"Yes."

"Look at the dial marked 'Fuel 1 Rate. That's the rate you've been using fuel during the last ten minutes."

"220 pounds per minute," said Daniel.

There was a short silence at the other end of the radio, as Krassnyansk struggled to remain composed.

"You're using way too much fuel," said Krassnyansk. "Advise you decrease speed to 400 knots."

"Okay. How do I do that?" asked Daniel. Krassnyansk gave him instructions.

Krassnyansk looked again at his screen and saw KRA 1025 had now advanced 380 kilometers inland toward Volgograd. "Why," he wondered, "Would terrorists want to hijack a commercial airliner and continue flying it to its originally scheduled destin—?"

"*Kak!*" he gasped, triggering his comm link on a new frequency.

"Borodin here," a voice came back on the link. It was Colonel Vassily Borodin, Deputy Commander of the Russian Air Force at Novorossiysk.

"Vassily, we have an emergency in Sector 18. Airliner KRA 1025 is headed on a course directly for Volgograd. Suspect hostile intentions, including hijacking," said Krassnyansk, as calmly as he could, given the huge implications if his suspicions were proven true.

"Hijacking? Uri, you've been drinking too much of that Ural Vodka. I told you to stay away from that stuff. Do you realize the mess you'll be in if you report this?" exclaimed Borodin.

"No, Vassily. I fully believe their intention is hostile. The man now flying the plane is a passenger because the terrorists killed the pilot and co-pilot. The passengers have miraculously re-taken control of the aircraft," explained Krassnyansk. "I checked with Ataturk RATCC when I became suspicious. Call them if you don't believe me!"

Borodin went off the air for a minute. When he returned, his voice was much more animated. "Uri, I have confirmed your story with Ataturk. Seems the hijackers were able to break into the cockpit and commandeer the plane."

"Vassily, I recommend you scramble your men immediately. There is a major oil refinery in Volgograd, with substantial natural gas holding capacity. The hijackers may have been targeting it all along. They might be Chechen separatists!" At this realization, both men froze for a split second.

"Kuyasye!" Holy shit. Borodin yelled. "The refinery has nearly 30% of all Russian oil-refining capability! This could be totally disastrous! I'm scrambling now. Uri stay close to the comm, and get the passenger to divert his aircraft. Have him land it at Rostov-on-Don. And wake up General Zaitzev. He must be brought into this immediately!"

Four minutes later, two MiG-29 fighters lifted off simultaneously from the Novorossiysk airfield, accelerating to 1500 knots. Each carried a contingent of four AA-11 'Archer' air-to-air missiles. The fighters quickly acquired an intercept course for KRA 1025 while Borodin advised Krassnyansk of an estimated intercept time of sixteen minutes from lift-off, positioning the strike point near

Volgodonsk, Russia. The lead pilot was Major Victor Ustinov, a fifteen-year veteran.

Both Russian commanders now relaxed slightly. They had done all they could, reacting to what appeared to be a major threat to Russian security and its economy.

Suddenly, Krassnyansk tensed again.. He fingered the comm link: "Vassily?"

"Borodin here," was the reply.

"Vassily, this is Uri. Uh,…I just had a terrible thought."

"What's that?"

"The RATCC at Ataturk said there were thirty-six Russians and one hundred fifty other passengers and crew on board. This must have been the terrorist's insurance policy, knowing we would hesitate to shoot down our own citizens!"

"Yes, and if General Zaitzev were here he would likely order the MiGs to shoot them down considering their proximity to Volgograd."

"I agree. But we don't have a choice. We would probably be court martialed if we don't inform Zaitzev."

"*Yob!* Call the airliner!" screamed Borodin. "Get them to divert, now. MiGs will be there in under fifteen minutes. A hundred and eighty six people are going to die if you don't get them out of there."

Krassnyansk yelled, "Popov", to a lieutenant seated two stations away.

"Yes, Commander?"

"Ask General Zaitzev to come here at once. Run. It is urgent!"

"KRA 1025, what is your current heading?" barked Krassnyansk into the airliner comm.

"Forty two degrees north," replied Daniel.

"Change immediately to course two-six-five. This will take you to the airfield at Rostov-on-Don, Russia." The Russian ATC took a minute and explained to Daniel how to change the airliner's heading.

"And one more thing, Daniel Prescott. There is danger headed your way!"

"What?" Daniel was surprised. What could possibly pose a greater danger than what they had been through already?

"We have analyzed your flight plan and believe your aircraft is headed directly for the refineries at Volgograd!"

Krassnyansk continued, "This facility is the largest in Russia, responsible for a substantial amount of our oil- and gas-refining capacity. I believe it was the terrorists' intent to fly the plane directly into the refinery, destroying it. It would take us years to re-build."

Daniel alterted Bill, "Of course! That's why the fanatics hijacked the airliner, knowing the military might hesitate to attack it because of Russian passengers."

Just then, an officer from the Russian Military Security Agency burst into the Novorossiysk control tower. "We believe we know who the terrorists are!" he shouted, waving copies of official-looking reports.

"They are likely a band of anti-Russian Georgians and Chechens, led by a fanatic named Giorgi Bakradidze. He had been suspected in several small attacks on Russian military and civilian personnel over the past five years. He had also gained considerable flying experience with

Georgian military transport aircraft, very similar to the big Boeing wide body planes such as the 767."

The officer continued to summarize the written reports while Krassnyansk scanned the documents marked "Top Secret."

According to the report, Giorgi was a suspect in the bombing of the train station in Krasnodar in 2006; known as a firebrand orator; and a suspected participant in the insurgency following the second Chechen war.

Krassnyansk paused over this, thinking, "Wasn't that the time of the Abkhazi uprising? Yes, it said his parents were murdered by Abkhazi gangs because of their underlying hatred of Georgian culture. No wonder this man had become a terrorist. He might be trying to avenge his parents' death, which he could have blamed on the Abkhazis and their Russian advisors in the Georgian-Abkhaz War."

Krassnyansk was about to return the documents to the security official when he noticed something odd. "It seems his father owned a small machine shop while he lived in Tbilisi. Strange for an academic. But, whatever!"

Momentarily distracted by the security official, Krassnyansk returned his attention to Daniel and KRA 1025.

"On the right side of your steering wheel there is a red button. Do you see it?" he asked.

"Yes."

"Push it."

Immediately there was a loud, low-pitched beeping. "Hey, what's that noise?" said Daniel.

"That's okay. Push it again," commanded the Russian.

Daniel did so and the beeping stopped. "It stopped," he exclaimed.

"Good," said Krassnyansk. "You are on manual control. You can now change course by turning the steering wheel in front of you. Turn it to the left until the electronic display reads '265.'"

Daniel turned the wheel counterclockwise. "Hey!"

"What's wrong?"

"Nothing's happening," Daniel reported.

"*Kak!*" said the Russian commander under his breath. "The terrorist must have locked in the course setting with a code!"

Krassnyansk barked, "I'm going to try something else, but I may need additional help."

"Whatever. Let's get…" Daniel stopped mid-sentence. "Oh, shit!"

"What is it?"

"MiGs! One on either side of me!" yelled Daniel.

At that moment Krassnyansk heard chatter from the lead MiG.

"Major Ustinov to Novorossyisk control."

"Yes, major. Commander Krassnyansk here."

"Airliner in sight now. Karaca Airlines markings, uhh, looks like a 767, uhh, and there's something strange…"

"What is it?"

"Airliner is trailing streams of vaporized liquid from both wing tanks. Estimate it is dumping fuel!"

"Roger. I'll advise the airliner pilot."

"Roger. We are climbing above the fuel streams now as they pose a danger to us when ignited."

Sweat broke out on Krassnyansk's forehead as he stole another glance at his screen. KRA 1025 was now only 300 kilometers from Volgograd. For the first time, he began to doubt whether the aircraft and passengers could be saved.

He reminded himself, "There are two vital tasks: stopping the fuel leaks and preventing the airliner from being shot down with an 'Archer' missle." Krassnyansk prioritized the greater danger first: divert the airliner from its present course.

"KRA 1025, Roger your sighting of MiGs. I will advise you on proper actions." Then added, "Do you see the electronic display where you just gave me a heading a moment ago?"

"Yes."

"Just below the small navigation screen there are three black buttons. Do you see them?"

"Yes.".

"Push the left button and try turning the wheel."

Daniel complied. "Nothing."

"Repeat, this time pushing the second button," Krassnyansk commanded.

"Again, nothing." Daniel tried the third button, with the same result.

"What could be their damn code?" Krassnyansk punished himself with the question. Everyone was despondent, knowing the airliner was doomed if they could not change course.

Just then, General Vassily Zaitzev, head of Black Sea Air Defense Operations, stormed into the Novorossiysk ATC tower. "What is it, Krassnyansk?" Quickly, the lieutenant commander briefed the general on the situation, including a summary of the security agent's report. The general's face turned grave and commanded an immediate communication with the Kremlin.

Everyone in the tower fell silent, attending only occasionally to their digital radar screens. General Zaitzev took a few moments, thinking intently to himself. Then he turned slowly to face the lieutenant commander.

"Commander, they are too close. It is hopeless," he said to Krassnyansk in a low voice.

"But, General…"

Zaitzev cut him off, anger rising in his voice, "Do you realize what the consequences are? This attack will cripple the Motherland for years, not to mention the loss of billions of Euros for natural gas from the Europeans. It must be done! Besides, we don't know if the man flying the plane isn't a terrorist himself. It could be a trick."

KRA 1025 was now only 280 kilometers from Volgograd.

The general grabbed the comm link to the MiG commander. "Major Ustinov, This is General Zaitzev. I am ordering you to shoot down the Karaca airliner. Now. That's an order!"

Stunned, the pilot hesitated momentarily. "Yes, sir. It will take me twenty seconds to maneuver for a shot." he replied to the general and ordered his wingman to accompany him to an appropriate firing distance behind the commercial jet.

"General, there are Russian civilians on that airliner!" yelled Krassnyansk, incensed.

Zaitzev countered, "You are out of line, Commander!" Then, to the sergeant-at-arms he bellowed: "Commander

Krassnyansk is to be restricted to the lobby area. Use your sidearm if necessary."

As he was led toward the outer lobby a helpless feeling came over the devastated commander. One that he hadn't experienced since he was a boy in his father's machine shop in St. Petersburg, where the milling machinery he was using went out of control, sending him into a panic until his father punched in a safety code on the machine's three buttons.

As he approached the lobby, Krassnyansk heard one of the ground controllers curse as he slapped an old style monochrome computer monitor, "***Gavno***! Shit! ***Nyet robota***! Doesn't work! Why is it asking for a code? What code?"

"Hey, Boris!" yelled another ground controller, laughing. "Why don't you use another one from the closet?" Laughter continued from the other men.

"***Nyet, Sovak***," said Boris. "They are all from old Soviet manufacture. All the same hardware and software. All the same codes. ***Kycochek Kaka!*** Piece of Shit!"

Krassnyansk froze, but his mind accelerated. "That's it!" he yelled to anyone who could hear. "*All the same codes.* That's it!" He grabbed the armed escort by the shoulders and shook him, temporarily distracting him.

"That's it. The equipment in Soviet-era machine shops was all the same! That means all their codes were the same! The machines all had three buttons for emergency shutoff, which means the terrorist probably used the same machines in his father's shop as my father did! That's where he could have created the code for the three buttons on the navigation display on the aircraft!"

92

MiG pilot Ustinov armed his first missile. "Missile is armed, general."

Krassnyansk, knowing he risked his own career and possibly his life,, tossed the guard aside and bolted back into the control room, pushing other people out of his way.

"Do you have a firing lock?" asked Zaitzev, who looked up at a wild-eyed Krassnyansk forcing his way into the room.

"Yes, general, locking on now," replied Ustinov over the comm.

Krassnyansk reached the comm to the MiG pilot and tried to push the ATC operator aside but several hands grabbed at his uniform to restrain him.

"Fire!" commanded Zaitzev.

With a huge effort Krassnyansk broke free of the constraining hands and yelled into the MiG comm link, "Stop!"

Surprised, the MiG pilot hesitated momentarily on his missile firing button.

The general was furious. "Commander Krassnyansk, do you know the penalties for insubordination? For treason?"

Ignoring the general, the lieutenant commander keyed the switch to the airliner comm link. "KRA 1025, under the navigation screen, push the left button once, the middle button twice, and the right button three times. In that order. Hurry!"

Bill, still in the co-pilot's seat, complied immediately, punching the three buttons in sequence. Daniel turned the yoke to port. There was a shudder and the entire aircraft vibrated for a second but the big Boeing airliner responded, lumbering steadily to the left.

"It's turning!" Daniel yelled back into the comm. "We're heading west to course 265!"

"General," MiG pilot Ustinov exclaimed, "Airliner is turning to port and is veering off the direct course to Volgograd! Their new heading is 265, toward Rostov-on-Don."

There was a huge pause in activity in the military ATC tower, like a pin could be heard dropping on the other side of the runway. Another ATC in the Novorossiysk control room confirmed the maneuver and nodded to the general.

General Zaitzev acted quickly. "Stand down, Major. Stand down. Do NOT fire, Repeat. Do NOT fire. You are to escort the airliner to Rostov-on-Don."

"Yes, sir. Affirmative. Standing down," replied Ustinov as he flipped the safety cover on his missile firing lever to a closed position. "Weapons are cold. Repeat. Weapons are cold," said Ustinov. He and his wingman fell back, taking up a defensive stance a half-kilometer behind the Boeing 767.

Cheers filled the control tower and the KRA 1025 cockpit. Krassnyansk buried his head in his arm and began to sob tears of gratitude. Zaitzev recognized that Krassnyansk belonged back at his post and ordered, "Commander, you may resume your duties."

"Yes, sir," Uri responded. "It was a long shot, but it worked."

Tears of joy appeared on many other faces at the Novorossiysk RACC, expressing relief at sparing the lives of thirty-six of their own citizens whom they swore to protect and serve.

"Now, Daniel Prescott," he spoke into the airliner comm link. "You have a fuel leak. To stop it press the red button just under the flap controls."

Bill spotted the button immediately. "That one," he barked to Daniel while pointing at the control panel.

"I see it. Pressing button now," replied Daniel.

The red light on the button turned off and the fuel jettison valves were closed by another redundant cicuit acting as a safety for the main fuel jettison control.

KRA 1025 was safe!

Krassnyansk instructed Daniel how to return to automatic pilot.

All that remained was to land at the nearest Russian airfield.

But that was a lot to ask for as his Boeing 767 was running dangerously low on fuel!

CHAPTER 10
Rostov-on-Don

✧

KRA Flight 1025
At 12,000 feet over Vesolyy, Russia.
August 10, 2008

"KRA 1025, we have identified an airfield that can accommodate your 767 aircraft," said Krassnyansk.

"Please advise," Daniel responded.

"Rostov-on-Don has an airport and they are 140 kilometers from your present position. To arrive at the airport come to a heading of 310 degrees," said the Lt. Commander. "I am transferring communications to the air traffic controller there, Major Dimitriyev. He knows the territory and the approaches better than anyone at Novorossiysk."

"Roger. Going to 310 degrees," said Daniel, as he maneuvered through the manual-auto pilot routine again. "Rostov Tower, please respond. How far are we from your airfield?"

As Krassnyansk relinquished comm control to the Rostov ATC, he had a sickening feeling but said nothing. He knew the runway at Rostov Airport was at least 150 meters shorter than the standard commercial airport runway. "May God be with them," he prayed silently.

"One Hundred Forty kilometers. One, Four, Zero," replied the Rostov ATC. "My name is Dimitriyev."

"I hope we can get that far," thought Daniel.

"You're powered back to 400 knots, correct?" asked Dimitriyev. "You should be able to make it. I'll advise when the airfield should be visible. Remember to keep your eye on the fuel gauge."

"Yeah," said Bill. "Pretty soon we'll be running on fumes."

"Roger," replied Daniel, looking left to give the instruments a critical eye.

Three minutes passed before a crackling came over the comm link. It was Dimitriyev.

"The Sea of Azov should be in view off to the left. It's the northern part of the Black Sea. The city is about 32 kilometers northeast of it."

Another ten minutes passed when suddenly a shudder, a jolt, and a rumbling. "What the heck was that?" yelled Daniel.

"We probably lost one of the engines," said Bill.

"Must be a fuel shutdown on one of the engines. Check the fuel readouts to the left of the center console," advised Dimitriyev. "Are they all red?"

Quickly Daniel checked the forward instrument board to the left of the yoke. "Yes."

"*Kak!*" thought Dimitriyev.

Then, addressing KRA 1025, "Let's hope you have enough fuel for a landing."

They were now fourteen kilometers from the Rostov airport, at about 1,000 meters above ground, 380 knots airspeed.

Another shudder, followed by a jolt. "There goes the port engine," yelled Bill.

"We're out of fuel. Can we glide in," asked Daniel over the comm. "Is there anything else we can do?"

"I'm afraid not. Your previous speed increase and fuel dumping has consumed fuel at a much faster rate," said Dimitriyev, with tension rising in his voice. "If you had the fuel you would push the throttles forward, pull the nose up with the yoke. That will maximize your lift. The flap controls are located above the altimeter. Fourteen kilometers to touchdown!"

"Bill!" yelled Daniel. "Bring the most experienced crew member to the cockpit!"

A minute later, Bill appeared in the cockpit doorway with Anika, a cute blonde flight attendant who had been with Karaca for four years. She had been a victim of Giorgi's initial assault.

"Do you know anything about the controls or gauges in the cockpit?" Daniel asked in desperation. "We need to go another fourteen kilometers to the Rostov airport but we're out of fuel."

"No," she replied. She pointed at the dials to Daniel's right. "All the fuel gauges are there, for both the engines. I don't know of any other…" as she trailed off, a first aid kit she'd been using to help the passengers slipped from her other hand, clattering to the cockpit floor. "Oh, sorry!"

She and Daniel reached simultaneously to recover the kit. Both their hands reached it at the same time. Anika grasped it, and as she began to draw it toward her, she noticed that Daniel's left hand had not moved. She glanced over at the strange expression on his face. Daniel's eyes were wild, as if he were in the path of a charging rhino.

"What the hell is that?" Daniel demanded, startling both Bill and Annika.

"What do you m—" Anika began to speak, only to be cut off by Daniel.

"R," he said. "Why is that button marked 'R?'"

No one answered. They were all thinking of only one thing: their aircraft had run out of fuel and they were going to crash.

"Why would there be a button marked 'R' underneath the fuel gauges?" Daniel wondered out loud, staring forward through the window, the ground beginning to come up rapidly below them, their altitude now a mere 500 meters above ground.

"I do not know," said Dimitriyev over the comm link, his voice dropping in intensity, almost to confirm acceptance their end was near. "But I'll ask our technical expert in the tower."

Their airspeed had dropped to 225 knots. Silence fell as they waited for death to take them.

Suddenly, Anika spoke, "It is for fuel! I heard the captain on another flight use this button once. It is, how do you say..."

"It's a *Reserve* button," yelled Daniel. "Bill, push it! Anika, tell the passengers to prepare for impact. Emergency!"

Bill dived for the reserve button, and a little blue LED light came on inside the fuel gauges for engine #1 and engine #2. "Try a re-start, both engines," he yelled.

"I have no idea how to start the engines. I can fly the aircraft with guidance from the ATC, once the engines have already been started."

"What was that?" a voice came over the comm link. Dimitriyev's.

"We think we have reserve fuel but don't know how to re-start the engines," Daniel responded.

"Easy!" yelled the ATC. "Just bring both throttles to neutral position—vertical on the levers—and hit the start buttons for each engine, located just above the throttles. One at a time. As soon as you feel each one engage, push the throttle forward to beat the hell!"

The 767 had descended to 100 meters above ground and reached the edge of a ravine 250 meters deep and one kilometer wide, just over one kilometer east of the airport. Airspeed was 150 knots. Only two kilometers to touchdown. So close, yet so far.

Anika grabbed the passenger mike and warned everyone on board to brace for impact in English, Russian and Turkish. Screams and tears met this announcement, and passengers began saying prayers.

Daniel's eyes were glued to the start buttons and throttles. He punched the start button for #1. A rumbling sound and slight shudder!

"That's it. Give her more juice," ordered Bill. Daniel complied. He repeated the process for #2, with the same result.

"Now pull the yoke up, push the flaps to maximum. It will gain altitude as long as airspeed is at least 140 knots," urged Dimitriyev. "And we were informed that some 767's are equipped with a special link between the aft auxiliary engine and the main wing tanks, for reserve fuel".

"Thank God it was done on this aircraft," breathed Bill. "Wonder how much fuel they contained…"

Still with a slow airspeed, the 767 descended into the yawning embrace of the ravine.

Daniel keyed the comm for what he believed was the last time: "Mayday, Mayday. This is KRA 1025, two kilometers east of Rostov airport. We are out of fuel and going down into a ravine. Send emergency vehicles."

Dimitriyev checked one more thing. "Do you have throttles at maximum?"

Daniel, totally preoccupied as imminent death confronted all of them, cried in desperation, "Wha… Yes, Yes. Engines are at redline RPM!"

The two General Electric engines whined ferociously and caused the entire aircraft to shake violently. Daniel used all his strength to hold the throttles at their maximum thrust position, the yoke in full retraction and the flaps at a maximum 40 degree setting.

Annika covered her ears and wedged herself in the doorway to gain her balance as the punishing vibrations continued. But the aircraft ceased its descent and began an upward trajectory as airspeed reached 150 knots, Several trees and shrubs caught fire, battered by the superheated engine exhaust raging in close proximity to the ravine's walls.

But a new problem arose. Daniel was suddenly distracted by a blaring cockpit alarm.

"Wha…what is that…?" he cried.

"Stall alarm!" Dimitriyev responded, "You have exceeded the stall angle of attack limit! Push the yoke forward but only part way. You still have to clear the ravine," he commanded.

An ATC in the Rostov tower called emergency rescue crews and advised their approach would involve getting around the steep ravine. It would be impossible to get any men directly down the sides due to the anticipated fire. "Maybe they can rig a number of rescue ropes…."

"No. There will be no rescue," said another ATC. "Remember the plane that went down about ten years ago? They couldn't even find the seat cushions. Everything was incinerated."

The tower's radio communications were being relayed to Novorossiysk, which in turn transmitted them to Defense HQ in Moscow, where a minor diplomatic genius keyed a link to his emergency diplomatic counterpart at the National Security Council at the White House. A half dozen NSC staffers were informed of the airliner's plight.

The controllers at Rostov continued to watch helplessly. The aircraft had disappeared from view. Everyone's heart sank like a stone. A couple of seconds passed. Everyone expected their next visual would be a huge fireball spilling over the west rim, setting the scrub brush ablaze. Another second. "Visual contact has been lost," an ATC said. Aides at the White House rapidly translated from Russian to English for the rest of the NSC staff.

Suddenly, one of the Russian ATCs noticed a rounded, silvery shape just beginning to appear behind the western edge of the ravine.

"My God, the force of the blast was so great it jettisoned the cockpit and nose cone assembly upward," said an ATC in a low voice, expecting a large explosion in the next second.

Instead, more silvery smooth surface made its way into visual range, then a sharp fin-like structure appeared behind it. "Wh...Wh...What is that?" the ATC yelled. "*Khuyasye*! It's the vertical stabilizer!" yelled another ATC.

Then the full shape of the 767 became visible.

"Oh my God, it's them!" he yelled in Russian. "They made it!" The room erupted in cheers and screams so chaotic that neither the Kremlin nor the White House could tell what was being said and thought they heard lamentations at the explosions and dead bodies.

Finally someone at the NSC center heard something recognizable, even though it came from 8,000 kilometers away: "Holy shit! They made it!"

The NSC center was in chaos, the noise so loud that the President halted another meeting three rooms away to check on the source, only to be dragged into the celebration.

"Rostov Tower, this is KRA 1025 on approach for an emergency landing. Tell me how to land this thing!" Daniel pleaded, as he pushed the nose down further and cut back on the throttles to bring the aircraft out of its upward, rocket-like trajectory.

Dimitriyev resumed his guiding presence. "You only have enough fuel for one pass, so we're bringing you in on this try—it's all for the marbles," he said in his accented English.

"You mean 'for all the marbles,'" corrected Daniel, smiling. This small bit of levity brought a few seconds' emotional relief to the exhausted American.

"*Da, da*. Yes. Yes. As you Americans say, 'for all the marbles,'" exclaimed the ATC, keeping the situation light-hearted.

Then he went back to business.

"Cut power back to thirty percent, and put the nose down so you can see the landing strip. Landing gear control is to the immediate right of the left control wheel, captain's side. Pull the lever down and confirm you have three green lights. This means the landing gear is locked."

"There are the levers," said Bill as he pointed to the right of the yoke on Daniel's side.

Daniel complied, and the 767's landing gear extended and locked. "Confirmed. Three green lights." The Karaca airliner slowed to 150 knots airspeed.

"Push the nose down just a touch more," the ATC instructed. "Good. Now remember, your wheels are six meters, ahh... nineteen feet, below where you are sitting. Begin your descent at 40% flaps. You will land by cutting speed, not by pushing the nose into the runway.

"Roger that," responded Daniel.

The runway was now 800 meters in front of him. Then 700. 600. 500. The big, 155 ton airliner slowed to 130 knots, its wheels were 25 meters off the ground.

"You're a little low," said the Russian ATC. "Increase thrust slightly. Keep your nose up, right where it is now. Keep a ten degree up-bubble on your attitude indicator. That's it. Good nose. Good speed. Cut back a little more. Remember you want to touch down with those big wheels under the wings."

"Airspeed 120," said Daniel, with a glance at the airspeed indicator.

"Good. You are at fifteen meters above the ground," said Dimitriyev. "Almost home. Pull back on throttles slowly but steadily. That's it. Cut back a little more. A little more. Good. Good."

The runway was now 150 meters away, 14 meters below the wheels.

"Rog..." but before Daniel could complete the phrase, a slight bumping motion and small rumbling vibrated the aircraft. "What was that?" Daniel asked.

"Ahh…I think..You just took out a half dozen lights on the approach gantry. No big deal. They can be easily replaced," said the Russian, trying to remain calm and supportive.

"We're going to stop by just using the brakes instead of the reverse jet thrust. I don't want to add any more complications to your job. Besides, you might run out of fuel and the reverse thrust would be useless anyway.

"The brakes are like automobile brake pedals and are under the display. Good nose. Good speed. Cut back a little more…Your approach is excellent. As soon as the wheels hit, bring your throttles back to zero. The nose will drop on its own, and you can use the brakes the rest of the way. You are just a few seconds away."

The tarmac was fifty meters in front of the Boeing aircraft. Then, forty, thirty, twenty… Airspeed one hundred, ninety-five, ninety… the wheel height above runway was five meters, four, three…

Bump… Then another bump…The main landing wheels had hit the tarmac.

Touchdown!

"Now," yelled the ATC. "Cut all power. Throttles in neutral."

Daniel pulled the throttles to neutral with what seemed like the last bit of strength in his wounded body. Bill leaned over to offer assistance with the throttles. The engines became silent. As if by a miracle, the nose began to drop forward. They were now hurtling down the runway at around eighty knots.

"Brakes," yelled Dimitriyev over the comm. "Use both your feet. Easy at first, then harder as I instruct you."

Daniel obeyed, applying easy pressure at first to the pedals below the control panel. Ground speed dropped to seventy-five knots. The nose came all the way down with a soft *Thunk!*

Dimitriyev yelled, "Now use the small steering wheel to the left of your seat to steer the nose wheel. Brakes! Again! Now more! Harder!"

Daniel pushed with his legs, increasing resistance every couple of seconds, while his left hand maneuvered the nose wheel steering mechanism. Ground speed dropped to seventy, then sixty knots. The aircraft shuddered slightly. Smoke billowed from the wheels as the brake pads became subjected to unusually intense pressure. Undeterred, Daniel maintained his focus on the pedals: fifty knots, forty, thirty, twenty, ten… Daniel eased up on the brakes. The 155-ton aircraft bobbed up and down twice, then came to a complete stop with fifty meters of runway to spare.

He had done it!

Dimitriyev pumped his fist and high-fived several fellow ATCs. Shouts and applause continued in the Russian control center for more than thirty seconds, normally a place with a stiff, dour atmosphere. The celebration was repeated in the NSC conference room.

Dimitriyev advised Daniel over the radio on how to shut down the engines, and Daniel complied. Also with direction from the controller, he maintained pressure on the brakes until ground crew outside indicated that they had chocked the wheels.

Then, everyone heard the roar of two MiG-29's overhead, as Major Ustinov and his wingman did a flyby, before settling into an easy landing on another runway, their approach facilitated by light winds.

Daniel was faintly aware of wild noise coming from the cabin, then realized it was cheering, crying, weeping for joy. Ecstatic passengers hugging complete strangers. Family members huddling together to weep for joy, and then embracing other families. Bill stood beside him and gave him a hug as best he could without touching his injured arm.

Anika embraced Daniel's head. Suddenly, Daniel was aware of this woman's comfort and her soft closeness.

Anika carefully held Daniel's left arm. "Let's see if we can make you a better bandage. You might need a sling, considering there are two flesh wounds. I have the first aid kit. Let me see your arm more closely."

The Rostov tower controller immediately redirected other aircraft to land on a cross runway, allowing KRA 1025 to remain in position.

The crew opened the main cabin door on the port side, and ground crews wheeled a step ramp up to the opening. Flight attendants welcomed the first security detachment with arms raised and screams and shouts of joy in English and Russian. The security men were overwhelmed.

"These passengers are crazed," they thought. "The terrorists must have tortured them." The passengers began to kiss the security team, pushing them back down the ramp. Everyone laughing, crying, smiling, screaming for joy. Thirty, fifty, then a hundred passengers spilled down the ramp and onto the tarmac, many kissing the surface as if it were holy ground.

Then they turned their attention to the security detail. Women grabbed the soldiers and planted big kisses on their faces, refusing to let go. The men resisted their military instinct to maintain control at all times, realizing this was for the good of all. It was a mad house, captured by photographers inside the terminal.

"We must get him to a doctor right away," commanded another flight attendant as four people carried Matt out the doorway to the top of the ramp. "Anyone speak Russian?" Immediately two passengers still on board responded and began yelling in Russian down the ramp for medical assistance. A small contingent of workers inside the terminal burst out with a stretcher to take Matt to a hospital.

The remaining passengers exited the Boeing jet and joined the others on the tarmac. The euphoria continued, as complete strangers embraced and talked at each other in completely alien languages. More laughter and crying. Then a notable hush enveloped the crowd.

At the top of the ramp stood Bill, Anika, and Daniel. All three were somber as medics with stretchers removed the bodies of the captain and co-pilot, who were both killed by the terrorists. The hush continued as the stretchers came down the ramp and entered the terminal building.

Then renewed commotion broke out again, accompanied by loud 'hurrahs' as Bill and Anika came down the ramp. They extended their hands to passengers all around. A buzz preceded them, as some passengers recognized them as having actually fought the terrorists or assisted in landing the aircraft. The noise built into a crescendo as passengers saw Daniel at the top of the ramp, his left arm in a sling. As he descended, some of the passengers actually tried to climb the ramp again to greet him, or simply to touch him. There was screaming, yelling, crying as he reached the bottom. Everyone was aware of his critical role in their survival.

"So this is the man, *Americanyetz!*" several people said in Russian. They tried to push closer to touch the man who defeated the terrorists and landed the plane, but security forces, fearing for Daniel's physical safety and noting his wounded arm, intervened, providing a protective escort for him into the main terminal. A crush of reporters awaited him, and the passengers on the tarmac chanted, "*Americanyetz, Americanyetz,*" American, American…

Before Daniel entered the terminal he inquired about his Turkish business partner, Tarkan, all but forgotten in the crush of life-and-death events of the past several hours. He was advised to wait a moment, then, from out of the crowd, he saw two security agents escorting his colorful friend toward him.

The two men embraced, tears coming down their faces, joyful that the other was safe. They spoke for a few moments before Daniel said, "We will catch up on everything later. But I may not be available for a while due to security debriefing procedures and the like. But we'll speak as soon as possible, even if you have to first return to Istanbul and I to the U.S."

Tarkan acknowledged this and gave his American friend one last hug and a grin. "You are crazy American guy!"

Meanwhile, Colonel Victor Mayanyetz, head of the small security detail, made announcements through a bullhorn, first in Russian, then in English. He instructed all passengers to enter the terminal via the door to the left of where Daniel had transited. There they would receive refreshments, give a quick debriefing to the security team, and be escorted by the team to one of the biggest and best hotels in the city.

"You will receive your luggage here after speaking just a few minutes with our agents. We will have several buses waiting to take you to the Hermitage Hotel, the best in town! Of course you are all guests of the Russian government. Your meals and lodging are 'on the house.' It is our honor to serve brave people such as yourselves.

"Also we have recovered your cell phones, passports, and computers which the terrorists stole from you. Give us a couple of hours and we will place them in a special location at the hotel where you can pick out which is yours. We wish all passengers to be able to communicate with their loved ones, so please let us know if you are having difficulty with your cell phones. We will help in any way we can.

"During your interviews be sure to advise our agents of the contact information for your families or loved ones. We will begin that process immediately. We invite all relatives or close friends to come to Rostov-on-Don as quickly as possible, both to see you and to participate in a special celebration we are planning for tomorrow afternoon."

While the other passengers were being briefly questioned, Daniel and Bill went through a debriefing by military personnel, representatives of the Russian Air Traffic Control service, and two officials from the American consulate at Rostov-on-Don.

A total of eight Russians attended this extremely confidential discussion. At the same time, two physicians and two nurses from the Rostov State Medical University examined Daniel's wounds and provided fresh treatment and bandages. Mindful of his exhausted state, the officials went about their business expeditiously, eliminating any hint of duplicate questioning or bureaucratic involvement, a rarity in Russian official circles.

Officials terminated their questioning of Daniel and Bill and took them to the Hotel Hermitage where the other passengers had been bused. However Daniel insisted they take a detour to the Rostov State Medical University to check on Matt's status.

Daniel and Bill arrived just as Matt came out of emergency surgery.

"Will he be alright?" asked Daniel? His wounds were not life-threatening, explained the surgeons. He had lost a lot of blood, but no vital organs had been ruptured. He would need several days of complete rest with 24-hour vigilance.

"We'll let him rest," said Bill.

Doctors had already notified the U.S. embassy and been in touch with family members about his prognosis. There was nothing more Daniel and Bill could do, except write

Matt an encouraging note and leave it for him to view, upon his exit from the recovery room.

Both men rejoined the motorcade to the hotel and were able to bypass most of the passengers to their private rooms. A high-security detail of four Russian Special Forces guarded their two rooms. They were served an extensive hot meal in Daniel's room, joined by Vladimir Vulgoyov, a military aide from the Kremlin, along with a major from the Russian air force, an official from Karaca Airlines, and Anika the flight attendant.

Daniel, only able to stay awake for twenty-five minutes to eat dinner, began to succumb to fatigue after so many hours of stress and action. Everyone, including Bill, recognized this and they rose to retire, allowing the American time to rest.

Anika lingered for just a few seconds to give Daniel an embrace, not only for his bravery but to comfort a pain she sensed in his emotional life.

His thoughts turned to Arianna again. "I wonder what she would think of my role in this crazy adventure? Would she change her image of me?"

Daniel barely had enough energy to crawl into bed.

Cedar Stream Architects, Inc.
Seattle
August 11, 2008

Ten thousand kilometers away, Arianna completed her weekly staff meeting and retreated to her office, where a blizzard of sticky notes appeared on her chair. "When it rains it pours. Can't *anyone* else take the ball on the Yates acquisition project? Do I have to coordinate everything?" Arianna Reynolds wondered out loud, leafing through the multi-colored Post-Its.

She slumped down in the chair. "No one wants to wait. Everything is a priority. Maybe I could put bars on the door and windows. That would take care of it." Her cell phone buzzed as it lay on her desk. Joan.

"Hi there," she tried to feign cheerfulness.

"Did you see the announcement?" asked Joan excitedly. "Were you watching the news twenty minutes ago?"

"Wha...what are you talking about? I haven't seen anything but pissed-off managers concerned their portions of PR aren't going to be properly represented."

"My God, Arianna," interrupted Joan. "It's him. Oh my God, it's him. He's the one! Look at the online news reports."

"What? Just a second. I'm going online..." Arianna tried to calm her nearly hysterical friend. "She is usually so together," Arianna mumbled to herself. "What is wrong with her...?"

She scrolled the news headlines on her browser. "Something about a hijacked airliner in the Russian boonies!. Joan, are you okay? There is just something about a group of Russians..."

Joan reverted to a calm demeanor. "Arianna. Who do you know who just left on a business trip to Istanbul?"

"Why ... Daniel," was the reply. "But that was..."

"And he and Tarkan had to take another flight to Russia for a meeting. Their plane was hijacked by Chechen and Georgian terrorists before he could reach Volgograd. He and several other passengers defeated, no, *killed*, all six hijackers.

Then he managed to fly the plane into southern Russia. And Daniel landed the plane just as it was running out of fuel!"

Arianna was stunned.

"The CNN website says the Russians are treating him as if he were a returning World War II hero. They are all over him with praise and gratitude! He saved the lives of about 180 passengers, including thirty six Russians. And if his plane would have reached its target a large portion of Russian oil and gas refining would have been put out of commission!

"They're flying him back to Washington, D.C. tomorrow to meet with the President and top government officials and will be incommunicado until security procedures can be established for his safety."

Completely baffled, Arianna could not reply or move. She was only able to scroll through more of the story on the website and thank Joan for her call and hung up. She thought deeply for several moments.

"I think it's wise to support him.. He needs someone who has been a close friend, for sure. The whole incident must have been extremely traumatic.

"Joan is right. Life is not just about careers. Its about building a future with someone else, someone who truly loves me. My grandmother died not only destitute but *alone,* with no community, no one who truly loved her."

She took another minute to see the bigger picture about her relationship with Daniel.

"Yes, Daniel *is* that kind of guy," Arianna reminded herself. "Look at the depth of our friendship. We've done so much together. We're always relaxed in each other's company. And he has always cared for my well being. Have I been so clueless for this long? He's been right in front of me all this time. I've just been taking him for granted! He must be different now, more assertive and aggressive, with dispatching those terrorists and all."

Office of Capricorn Solutions, LLC
Seattle
August 11, 2008

"Peter, Ashley, **LOOK!!!**" yelled James from Marketing. "Look at the newsfeed!" As several employees crowded around James' computer screen there was a collective **"GASP"** as massive headlines appeared across the CNN website:

"Seattle Businessman Defeats Hijackers, Lands Plane. All Passengers Safe!"

"Wh…,? Oh my God!" several employees said at once. Some began to read the detailed CNN story out loud amid shouts from others viewing their screens…

"Entrepreneur Daniel Prescott, President of Seattle-based Capricorn Solutions, was instrumental in foiling the actions of six hijackers onboard a Karaca Airlines Boeing 767 headed for Volgograd, Russia. Prescott, 42, one of 181 passengers on board was held hostage with other travelers until he was able to free himself, and, while wounded, succeeded in acquiring terrorist weapons and shot his way into the cockpit of the aircraft, killing all six terrorists in the process. The hijackers had already killed the pilot and co-pilot and Prescott was able to safely land the

plane at Rostov-on-Don, in southern Russia while dangerously low on fuel. In fact, the aircraft was out of fuel on touchdown, according to Russian media sources. It is believed Prescott had no prior flying experience..."

All Capricorn employees continued to ramble about their leader for the rest of the morning, frantically phoning and texting relatives and friends to watch the news.

Around mid morning Peter received a phone call from State Department officials giving further insights into the incident and advised that Daniel sustained very minor injuries and was being taken to a hotel in Rostov-on-Don in the southern part of Russia to meet with Russian government and military officials.

Ashley noted, "Hey, maybe we should all take up meditation if this is the result? Wow, six hijackers and landing a plane that's running out of fuel? Maybe Daniel will give us free lessons or meditation time in the middle of the work day?" She traded high fives with several other employees.

Peter thought, "If only we could hold things together here for a few more days. When Daniel gets back we might get a break from a loan with a bank that wants to do business with a new American hero..." Peter's thoughts trailed off as he contemplated the financial squeeze still threatening the company.

CHAPTER 11

The Russians Are Coming!

Hermitage Hotel
Rostov-on-Don, Russia
August 11, 2008

Daniel awoke from a long sleep and found breakfast waiting for him in his room, along with Bill Casey and Colonel Vladimir Vulgoyov, a member of the Kremlin military liaison with the U.S. National Security Council. Vulgoyov, who participated in their brief dinner the night before, brought them up to speed on military developments in the Caucasus.

Before he launched into that conflict, Vulgoyov said, "Daniel, a diplomat from the U.S. embassy in Moscow is on his way to meet with you and someone from the Canadian embassy will be here for Bill. It will likely be sometime this afternoon. He asked that you prepare to return to the U.S. immediately, for security as well as other reasons. Bill, I assume the same will be true for you to return to Canada."

Daniel and Bill nodded acknowledgement.

Knowing his office and the GRU had already vetted the American and Canadian with extensive background checks overnight, Vulgoyov continued:

"I wanted to let you know of recent international developments since you've been occupied with other matters recently. The war with Georgia has been incredibly tense with hundreds killed on both sides, but our troops and special forces appear to be in control now." He proceeded to relate the latest results from the five-day war.

"Some things about the war are classified but since the two of you were instrumental in the defeat of the Georgian and Chechen hijackers, I can tell you that your actions likely held off more bloodshed than you can possibly imagine.

"As you may know, the Georgians have been taking aggressive action toward a number of ethnic Russian populations in Abkhazia and South Ossetia for several years. These people asked Russia to intervene to protect them and their property from destructive and discriminatory actions. Because they represent approximately 70% of the population in these provinces we could not turn a blind eye. You must understand."

"Of course," replied Daniel.

"Georgia became even more aggressive when it applied to join NATO. This action, if successful, would have trapped Russia in a no-win situation, and we would have been forced to take military action anyway. As it was, the Georgians attacked these people first. We were forced to respond. While Georgia had the element of surprise, our forces were able to capture and then exploit a key transit position through the Caucasus Mountains, the Roki

Tunnel, allowing sufficient troops and military equipment to rapidly disperse the attackers and hold the upper hand in South Ossetia."

Again, Daniel acknowledged his understanding of the grave situation, "Your military *had* to respond to both the aggression and to protect the vulnerable bottleneck of that tunnel."

"Precisely," confirmed Vulgoyov, as he walked to the window and gestured emphatically with both hands. "There were enough Russian tanks, artillery, and soldiers, assisted by Russian Special Forces, to achieve victory, and the Georgian troops have been chased all the way back to Gori, a provincial capital and site of a Georgian military base. So the war is essentially over.

"Although your U.S. Special Forces, including the Navy SEALS, receive more attention as the best all-around clandestine strike team, our Special Forces are not to be discounted," continued Vulgoyov with just a hint of a smile. "Just a few months ago we allowed NATO to observe a three day special military exercise near St. Petersburg. They all went away puzzled at how to counter the stealth and operational success of our Special Forces teams."

"Impressive," noted Bill. "I wouldn't want to go up against those guys!"

"And now I must tell you something that my government does not wish to make public. I ask you to maintain this in confidence. We don't yet know whether the hijackers were acting alone, out of revenge, or were part of an overall Georgian offensive plan. We suspect it was the former, as the lead hijacker, Giorgi Bakradidze, was a notorious critic of Russia who has been suspected of prior acts of sabotage against our country, even in peacetime."

Daniel got goose bumps as Vulgoyov continued, "It seemed that Giorgi was able to gain control of your airliner and lock his desired destination into the avionics system, so that navigation could only take place with a process he alone was able to control with a coded algorithm. His target, as you may have guessed, was Volgograd."

"But," Daniel wondered, "Volgograd is a civilian city. There are no military objectives…"

"They were not after military objectives," interrupted Vulgoyov. "Gentlemen, it is our belief that the airliner was locked on to a particular position in Volgograd at the very center of an oil-and-gas refinery complex on the southeast side of the city.

"Had the aircraft struck its intended target, perhaps 30% of Russian energy-refining capability would have been destroyed or severely damaged. These energy sources are vital for the economic well-being of Western Europe and several East European nations. There would have been several years of energy and economic catastrophe. The loss of foreign exchange into the Russian treasury alone would have amounted to several hundred billion Euros. If Commander Krassnyansk had not deciphered the code, the contingent of MiGs would have destroyed your plane to prevent this, and the death of 181 passengers and five crew members would have ensued.

Daniel and Bill glanced at each other and Bill whistled, "Wow. That was close!"

"Yes," continued Vulgoyov. "If the terrorists had been successful in their objective, the intensity of the current conflict with Georgia may have reached disastrous proportions. The Russian military would likely have demanded and executed the complete destruction of all Georgian forces and much of its civilian infrastructure in retaliation. We owe you and Uri Krassnyansk, the air traffic controller at Novorossiysk, a great deal of gratitude."

Daniel knew of the refineries at Volgograd from his communication the previous day with the ATC. But he had not known his airliner was locked on to the refineries as targets, nor how easily the war could have escalated. He couldn't speak for several moments.

"One more thing," said Vulgoyov. "Daniel, Bill. It is likely the terrorist organization that planned this attack, named *Irbis*, or Snow Leopard, is not completely defeated and may investigate and execute ways to harm you or friends and loved ones in reprisal attacks. We recommend you follow security measures, most likely to be offered by your governments, for at least the next six months."

Finally, Daniel managed to say, "Thank you, colonel, for that recommendation. Yes, I will follow up on security discussions with my government." Nodding at his companion he added, "Bill?"

Bill acknowledged Daniel's comment with a "Will do."

Daniel summarized their miraculous escape, "Had Commander Krassnyansk not broken the terrorists' code, the refinery might have been in ashes, and we would not be having this discussion."

"Yes, ahhh …that would be *Colonel* Krassnyansk, as we shall soon see. He is being promoted," noted Vulgoyov.

"Really?" exclaimed Daniel. "I would like to offer him my congratulations."

"You will be able to do so. One moment, please." Vulgoyov opened the door and commanded the Special Forces guard to bring in a guest. They waited as a tall, blond-haired man in a commander's uniform entered the room. Well-built, with an intelligent face and eager eyes, Commander Uri Krassnyansk turned, as if by instinct, toward Daniel first and offered a crisp salute.

"*Spaciba*. Thank you, Daniel Prescott. You have saved the Russian Federation. I congratulate you for your bravery and am grateful for your tenacity."

Daniel stepped forward and grasped the commander's right hand in a firm and sincere handshake, all the while looking into Uri's eyes with feelings of admiration and gratitude. "No," he countered, "it is you who have saved us. We owe you our lives."

Then Daniel embraced the Russian officer. Krassnyansk returned the gesture briefly, believing he should still maintain military decorum.

Krassnyansk then introduced himself to Bill, also with a firm handshake.

"You shall get a chance to visit with each other in a little while. But now, the Commander and I have some important business to attend to, as soon as our special guest arrives," said Vulgoyov, noting the surprised look on the faces of both Daniel and Krassnyansk.

"Here are our visitors," continued Vulgoyov. "It's time for all of us to meet the brass! Relatives of some of the passengers have arrived also. They will be anxious to see their loved ones. Daniel, Bill, please put on these suits which we have acquired for you. I trust the tailor who came to see you this morning has made a good fit."

Three buses full of civilians pulled up in front of the hotel. About eighty people, relatives of the passengers, were guided to the ballroom of the hotel's conference facility. They were kept at one end of the room, which had been cleared of chairs and tables. Bill and Daniel rose to follow Vulgoyov. Daniel was still a bit self-conscious with his left arm in a sling and endured numerous stares from Russian officers.

Daniel and Bill also noted the number of Russian military officers had doubled in just a few minutes. "Looks like they are rolling out quite a big carpet for Krassnyansk," Daniel surmised.

"Daniel, Bill, please follow me," urged Vulgoyov. "Commander, I believe you are wanted downstairs for, ahhh… questioning." Krassnyansk shook Daniel and Bill's hands one more time and strode briskly away.

Vulgoyov led Daniel and Bill to a special room on the main floor of the hotel. Several Russian officers accompanied them, most of colonel rank and above. Just as they were all about to enter the room, there was a big commotion in the hotel lobby, and at least a dozen of the military types sprang into action outside the hotel.

"This way, please," said Vulgoyov, as he ushered Daniel and Bill into the first of six rows of chairs which faced a small stage. The other rows were already occupied with military officers and three members of the Russian press.

"Gentlemen, please remain standing," said Vulgoyov in a low voice, taking a position beside them. Daniel and Bill looked puzzled but did as advised and remained quiet. "Too bad I have to wear this blasted sling another day," Daniel groused.

Suddenly a side door opened and five officers, four of them generals, entered the room. The generals were distinguished from the others by the rows of medals on their chests and their unmistakable look of command. Daniel and Bill immediately recognized the fifth officer. It was Krassnyansk.

"This must be his promotion ceremony," Daniel thought. He suspected one of the generals with the highest ranking would do the honors. But to his surprise all four generals lined up to the right of the Russian commander and stood at rigid attention.

All of a sudden, someone at the door made a loud announcement in Russian and every military man snapped to a smart salute.

Daniel gasped as a short but important-looking man entered the room, followed by several men in suits.

"Vladimir Putin, Prime Minister of the Russian Federation!" realized Daniel. "Holy smokes!"

Putin ascended the small stage, accompanied by a general and a colonel. The colonel held a small box of highly-polished wood. The military gathering dropped their salutes in one well-coordinated movement, and the general launched into a short speech while a single photographer maneuvered for appropriate angles. The speech in Russian could not be understood by either Daniel or Bill, but they caught Krassnyansk's name at the tail-end.

"Commander Uri Krassnyansk," the general called out.

Krassnyansk rigidly stepped away from the four generals who accompanied him and mounted the stage, standing directly in front of the lead general and crisply saluting him. The general returned the salute. The general then moved two steps to the side and Putin faced Krassnyansk.

A short speech by Putin followed.

When he finished, Putin motioned to the nearby colonel carrying not one, but two wooden boxes. He handed Putin the smaller box first. Meanwhile, the attending general approached Krassnyansk and removed his commander-rank insignia pins. Putin then pinned on the new insignias, each a golden bird shape, the rank of colonel.

While the Prime Minister stood in front of Krassnyansk, the second colonel approached, holding the other wooden box. From it Putin retrieved a golden medal with a navy blue neck ribbon. He placed it around Krassnyansk's neck and said, "Colonel Krassnyansk. You have performed bravely in the face of danger. Your actions saved many lives and spared our country much grief. This is the Medal of Malaya Zemlya, named after the heroic defense of Novorossiysk against the Nazis in 1943. It is given to officers in recognition of exceptional judgment and leadership."

Putin took one step back and stopped. The general barked a command for all officers in the room. Immediately all saluted as the general spoke. "Congratulations, Colonel Krassnyansk. You are a hero of the Russian Federation. Your name will be recorded in history associated with greatness." All dropped their salutes and applauded.

Krassnyansk did an about-face and walked briskly to an empty chair in the first row, three seats to Daniel's left and remained standing. All became quiet. "Now what?" wondered Daniel.

Putin stepped forward, and in heavily accented but precise English, said, "Daniel Prescott. William Casey."

"Uh-oh," thought Daniel. "I thought the ceremony was over. Guess not." Daniel took one step forward and positioned himself directly in front of Putin, feeling self-conscious with his arm in a sling in a room filled with military men. Bill followed him, and the American and Canadian now stood motionless before the Russian leader.

Putin then gave a short speech in Russian, recounting highlights of the previous day, including a summary of the hijackers' plot, the threat to civilian refineries in Volgograd, the scrambling of MiG fighters, the conflict on board the airliner in which Daniel and Bill were victorious, and the initiative of Krassnyansk.

He concluded by saying there was no award high enough to honor the men who, with passengers' help, defeated the Georgian and Chechen terrorists during a time of war. He asked the officers present to honor Daniel, Bill, and wounded Matt Carpenter with a salute and promised to introduce them to the Russian parliament.

A command was given in Russian and all in the room snapped to a salute, including Putin!

Daniel was in a state of semi-shock and continued to stand at attention, looking straight ahead at the Russian Prime Minister. Putin continued in Russian, with a quick transition to English for Daniel's benefit.

Putin concluded, "And now, Mr. Prescott, Colonel Krassnyansk and I go to meet the relatives of the passengers who have braved a difficult journey. Mr. Casey, please join my officers in the press area in the ballroom next door."

Putin motioned for Krassnyansk and Daniel to accompany him, while the remaining military men and Bill followed. Daniel and Putin were led to a large ballroom where the passengers and their relatives had been visiting each other for the past thirty minutes, still babbling away with tears and laughter.

Putin, Daniel, and Krassnyansk shook several passengers hands, then Putin and Daniel stepped back from the crowd.

"Mr. Prime Minister," Daniel said in a low voice, leaning toward Putin. "There is a special passenger in this room I think you should know about. It is a twelve-year-old boy. He was able to shoot one of the hijackers and helped us dispatch the others. Had it not been for his bravery, the hijackers would have gained the upper hand, and we would all have been killed. His name is Bobby Andrews. He is the small boy over there to the right, standing with his father."

Putin was surprised but retained his famous placid demeanor. "By all means. We should greet him now." He signaled the nearest security aide to come closer and instructed his team to bring the boy and his father forward.

Putin called his nearby security force to attention. Instantly eight Russian military aides and security men snapped to a rigid pose and saluted.

Putin approached the boy and said in English, "I have been advised of your bravery. Your actions have saved the lives of all these passengers and have averted a huge catastrophe for Russia and the rest of the world. On behalf of the Russian Federation, I offer you my thanks." Extending his hand, he warmly shook Bobby's, then his father's. "We shall meet again." Then Putin nodded and the security team dropped its salute.

As they departed the chatty scene in the ballroom, Putin asked Daniel to come to Moscow for a day of recognition, celebration and a few meetings.

Daniel agreed but said that he had been advised to return to Washington, D.C., for consultations with the President.

"Very well. We'll do it soon after you have taken care of business," said Putin.

They shook hands vigorously, knowing it wouldn't be long before they saw each other again. "By the way, did you know that three of the families of passengers are from Georgia?" asked Putin.

"No, I didn't know that!" remarked Daniel. The two men exchanged glances.

Daniel turned to leave for a meeting with the U.S. Counsel. "Good-bye, Mr. Prime Minister It's been a pleasure."

"Likewise," said Putin, who joined his military advisors for a return trip to Moscow.

Office of Anatoly Boyureck
Builder / Developer
Istanbul, Turkey
August 11, 2008

News of the thwarted hijacking spread quickly throughout the world and reached Anatoly's Istanbul office.

"Bok!" Shit! Thought Anatoly who had been certain the *Irbis* team would be successful. Now he had to formulate a backup plan, one that would send a strong message to the Kremlin about the strength of the terrorist team.

Keying on the American hero who disrupted the *Irbis* plans Anatoly directed his small staff to research connections to Daniel's Capricorn Solutions business and that of his Istanbul partner, Tarkan Kirni who's company, Bilgi, was located in Istanbul.

Later that day the staff's research began to pay off.

One of his assistants, Abir, approached Anatoly's office and said, "Mr. Boyureck, I have some discoveries that may interest you."

"Yes, yes. Come in, Abir"

"It seems Tarkan Kirni, Daniel Prescott's Turkish business partner, is also a mountain climber and belongs to a local climbing club. I spoke by phone to someone I know who is also a member of this club who occasionally meets Tarkan and other club members for refreshment in the evening. He has learned of an established friendship between Tarkan and a man named Mustafa who is part of a Russian climbing club. They have done several climbs together this year."

"Interesting," mused Anatoly. "Go on"

"Mustafa is fluent in Turkish as well as Russian and is located in Istanbul at this very moment.

"My friend also mentioned Tarkan has, for some time, been boasting about a proposed climb with his American partner, who is also a climber, about climbing together in the Alps this month.

Anatoly sat up straighter in his chair at this news. "Did he mention specifically their proposed destination?"

"Yes. They plan to climb the Matterhorn in southern Switzerland. However, Mr. Prescott was injured in that hijacking attempt a couple of days ago, so my friend doesn't know if the climb will continue as planned."

Anatoly bolted from his chair, "Do you have contact information for this Mustafa fellow?"

"Yes. Here are my notes. Oh, one more thing. My friend has learned Daniel Prescott has a special female friend, Arianna Reynolds, in Seattle. He favors her above all others."

Taking the notes from Abir's hand Anatolly extolled, "You have done well Abir! Please, take the rest of the afternoon off."

"*Tesekkur ederim.* Thank you Mr. Boyureck."

When Abir had left Anatoly closed his office door and placed a call to Mustafa's number as provided in his assistant's notes, and succeeded in arranging a coffee meeting with him the next day.

Anatoly placed another phone call to a friend at the Turkish foreign service and scheduled a dinner meeting with him for the next evening.

"Perhaps all is not lost," he said to himself, smiling.

CHAPTER 12
Mr. President, Madam Secretary

The White House
Washington, D.C.
August 13, 2008

The President, with the Secretary of State on
speakerphone, was given a morning briefing by the Secret
Service on their investigation of Daniel. They were joined by
William McKay, from the President's Council of Economic
Advisors.

"No criminal record. Nothing unusual from FBI, NSA
or CIA. Looks like he's been a successful entrepreneur for
several years and has a Ph.D in Computer Science. Seems
he was traveling to Volgograd just to meet with his Turkish
business partner's banker, looking for an expansion of credit,"
said Robert O'Neil, an investigative secret service agent.

"Not surprising," said McKay. "Millions of small
businesses are having trouble getting loans or any form of
banking credit because of the current financial situation."

"Pays his taxes on time every year," O'Neil continued.
"Looks solid to me."

"Thanks, Bob," said the President.

"Good work Bob," said the Secretary of State at the other end of the line.

McKay broke in, "You know, we've been working on a small business assistance program for a year now with Treasury, Commerce, and the Fed. We've figured most of the details of how it would work.

"If we had a champion helping us to promote the program, some nationally known businessperson…"

"Like Daniel Prescott," concluded the President.

"Exactly," confirmed McKay.

"Before he gets into that can I have him for a few days to do a little PR work with the Turks?" asked the Secretary of State.

"Sure, no problem," replied the President. "These programs won't be ready for a few months anyway. And we still need congressional approval."

Two hours later, Daniel was escorted to the Oval Office, no longer needing his sling, and extended his hand to the President.

The President took the lead. "Mr. Prescott, It's a pleasure to meet you. You've had a busy week to say the least. Welcome to Washington," shaking his hand and making introductions when they were joined by McKay and an undersecretary from Commerce.

"Thank you, Mr. President," said Daniel.

"No, thank you. If it hadn't been for your quick action the world would have been in quite a mess."

"I'm just glad I could help out."

"Help out? I should say so," said the President with a smile as he motioned Daniel toward a chair.

"Yeah, it was quite an ordeal," Daniel said with a chuckle, breaking the formality of their meeting ever so slightly.

"Well, I'd like to hear more about it," the President continued, "especially since you're the owner of an education software company, right?"

"Yes, in fact my Turkish partner and I were traveling from Istanbul to Russia to see a banker when the plane was hijacked, and, I…uh…guess you know the rest of the story."

"My staff told me some things," responded the President, "But I wanted to hear how you were able to take care of those hijackers. By the way do you mind if I call you Daniel?"

"No, not at all," said Daniel. "I sometimes wonder how it all happened, myself, Mr. President. I realized if I didn't use all of my skills to the very best I could, I wasn't going to get off that plane and neither were any of the other 180 passengers. I suspected they were going to try a 9/11-style attack when we continued to keep the same course."

"Good thinking, Daniel. Did you get help from the other passengers?"

"Absolutely. An older woman seated next to me was able to slip me a plastic knife and fork. I just became creative with those tools and was able to wrestle one of their weapons away and beat them at their own game."

"A deadly terrorist organization beaten by a plastic knife and fork! You're a pretty special guy, Daniel. The world owes you a lot."

"Thank you, Mr. President. I also had a lot of help."

"Thank the good Lord for them, too. Well, I was hoping to hear about your business as well. How's it going?"

"Until a few days ago my business was doing great," said Daniel. "But I've run into a cash crunch due to actions from a big customer. When my existing bank would not expand my line of credit, I flew to Istanbul to see if my Turkish partner could have more luck. Unfortunately, we couldn't consummate a deal with the Turkish bank because our airliner was hijacked."

McKay glanced at the President before addressing Daniel. "Yes, this is a huge problem for several million small businesses in the U.S. Since they can't get access to new capital due to this growing financial crisis, they are unable to expand. Since they can't expand, they also can't hire new employees, and our unemployment situation gets worse."

"Yes," said Daniel. "If I can't meet my customer's demands, he will go to another supplier, a bigger outfit. I won't be able to compete and I may have to lay off thirty-six people!"

"Daniel," the President broke in, "we are working on a new program that may address this problem. It involves having the federal government give more support to banks that provide expanded credit to small businesses. Now that we're having financial and credit jitters due to failures on Wall Street, all of our commercial banks appear to be backing off doing any major expansion of credit, even to top-notch small business customers who have consistently hit their numbers and have an strong credit history."

"We're thinking that Treasury, Commerce, and the Fed could work together on this—act as a guarantor of new lending, up to a certain limit, for a company that has been in good standing with its bank since before the crisis escalated this year," added McKay. "We're discussing it with the big commercial banks right now."

Daniel jumped in, "Sounds good, Mr. President. We've hit our banking covenant requirements every quarter. We could sure use a shot in the arm with credit."

McKay continued, "And we might allow banks who play ball on this to get some relief on reserve requirements. It's going to take a lot of work, but we've got to help our small businesses get back on their feet."

"Daniel," the President paused. "This program could help several million small businesses avoid a lot of difficulty, invest more in R&D, and start hiring again. After all small businesses account for 70% of all new hires."

Daniel nodded.

"I apologize for sounding opportunistic, but with your new visibility and popularity with the public, if you were a supporter of this program it would…I mean…we could really make this thing a 'Go.' We're hoping you could be a spokesman for us, just for a couple of months. And you wouldn't be doing this for free, of course"

Everyone smiled at the mention of this subtle 'job offer'.

"And why don't big, publically-traded companies do more hiring?" asked Daniel.

"Oh, they do hiring alright, it's just that most of it is done overseas in developing nations," McKay replied. "What they do a lot of in the U.S. is acquisitions and stock buy-backs, which actually *decreases* innovation, R&D, and overall domestic employment."

Daniel lamented, "Why am I seeing a disconnect between the objectives of capitalism represented by shareholder's interests, and employment and prosperity represented by workers' interests? It's exactly the opposite of the way it should be. It's like the capitalists' greed is restricting hiring. There should be laws against that!"

The President and McKay allowed themselves a slight smile. "You're right, Daniel," noted McKay. "We have a lot less 'free market capitalism' than most people realize. We have much more 'oligopolistic capitalism', dominated by a small number of large businesses. However, I don't think we can attack that particular shortcoming in the near-term.

"We think you are in a position to give this program a real boost," said the President, "as a high visibility spokesman."

Daniel was floored. "I'd love to help but I have a business to run. There are thirty-six employees and a couple dozen customers depending on me."

"We realize that," said the President. "What if we could assist you in dealing with your current payment-terms problem?"

"That would be awesome," said Daniel, "but how…?"

"Let's just say we have ways," said McKay.

"Good," said the President. "But why don't you take a few weeks off and think it over? Let your COO handle things, assuming we can get your financing straightened out."

"Fair enough," replied Daniel. "And thank you for offering assistance to my company. I really appreciate it." Then McKay rose to leave the Oval Office.

When just Daniel and the President were left in the room, the President closed the door for one last word.

"We and the rest of the world owe you a great deal of gratitude. I'll understand if you don't want to take this further. I think the task would suit you well. You have national and international recognition. You're a small businessman. And you appear to think fast on your feet. We really could use a guy like you."

"Thank you, Mr. President," Daniel replied. "You're very encouraging, and it certainly is an exciting opportunity to be at the forefront of a jump-start to the U.S. economy."

"Well, the opportunity is there for you. Just say the word. It reminds me of a phrase I once heard when I was trying to decide about making a significant career move into politics."

"What was that, Mr. President?"

"We can choose to play with mud pies in the alleyway, or build sand castles on the seashore. I guess I just wanted the bigger horizons that came with the seashore," he laughed.

Daniel joined in with a laugh of his own, "I guess you did! And I'm glad you did, Mr. President. Thank you for meeting with me. It's been quite an experience. I will consider your offer. And thank you again for taking the initiative to assist my company. There will be a lot of happy people if we're successful."

"My pleasure, Daniel. By the way, I believe the Secretary of State would like to see you as well. We've made all the arrangements for you and she will likely mention several security concerns about your protection. Secret Service agent, Jim Fowler, will escort you there."

"Yes, I'd be honored," said Daniel.

They shook hands and said their goodbyes. Then Daniel was escorted to the North Portico exit of the White House by Agent Fowler, a tall man with a moustache, a pleasant face, and a business-like demeanor. "This way, sir," he said, as he directed Daniel to a waiting black limousine.

Department of State
Washington, D.C.
August 13, 2008

"Yes, yes. Send him in," commanded the Secretary of State, when notified Daniel had arrived outside her office.

"I know I'm not the first to welcome you home, but I know I'm one of the proudest. So nice to meet you Mr. Prescott."

"Thank you, Madam Secretary, and it's my pleasure to meet you," he replied warmly, as he shook hands.

"Very well. Please, sit down," she said cordially. She introduced Daniel to several of her aides then signaled for them to be left alone for awhile.

"Well, looks like you've seen some action lately. And the Russians sure acted swiftly. It can take up to several days for me to get Putin's attention on a routine matter. Yet you get a private audience overnight! Maybe you'd be interested in signing on to my Russian liaison staff," she chuckled.

"Well, I'm a little overwhelmed at the moment. I wouldn't want to be signing on for an important task like that without giving it due consideration," said Daniel diplomatically.

"Just joking," she laughed. Then she turned to business. "I'm sure there are a ton of things the White House has on its agenda for you, the President has briefed me on his conversation with you. However, I know you must be exhausted and need a few weeks off. And, you still have a business to run, right?"

"I think you've been reading my mind," was his reply.

"Yes, of course. I thought we might talk for a little while, and then I'd like to have a private lunch with you and Alan Turnbull, my Under Secretary for Turkey and the Mideast. We'll get to the Russians later. Besides, I think you've just left them in a good position."

"Yes, I'd be honored, Madam Secretary."

"The honor is all ours," she said earnestly. "What I wanted to talk about were two major things. You have provided our country with some marvelous opportunities to make some international accomplishments that ordinarily might have slipped through our fingers.

"The first is with Turkey. This country has been doing great recently. Economically they've had very strong growth for several years and are well-positioned to increase their economic presence on the world stage while the Western countries are still hobbled by this growing credit crisis, a condition that's likely to last as long as ten years."

Daniel nodded his understanding.

"Secondly, their government appears to be strong and they are continuing to grow their democratic institutions. They have been a solid anchor for the Muslim world during a restive period in the Middle East."

The Secretary of State continued, "We have cordial relations with the Turks right now. But Daniel, it has not been lost on the Turks that your act of heroism saved the lives of some thirty-one Turkish passengers on board that Karaca Airlines flight. The Turkish press is all over it and is playing you up as a big-time hero."

"I was just in the right place at the right time, Madam Secretary," said Daniel, over-playing modesty just a little.

"That's not what I hear," replied the Secretary, smiling. Facing those automatic weapons and all. And flying that plane running out of fuel!"

"I was assisted by some very alert people and…"

"I heard all about it, Daniel. Lets give credit where its due!"

"You are really getting some great kudos. We've been monitoring a number of reports saying there has been an increase in pro-American sentiment as a result. This is good news for us as Alan Turnbull will elaborate on at lunch."

Daniel was impressed at this turn of events so quickly after the hijacking. "I'd be glad to help in any way I can."

"I appreciate that. And yes, there is a way you can help us further. We would like to position you as a businessman just trying to help the Turkish economy grow, especially its technology sector. During the next year we'd like to promote you to speaking at a few Turkish business and education forums where you would continue to maintain high visibility with the Turkish business community."

"What?" exclaimed Daniel. "You gotta be kidding."

"Just a half dozen times for a year. The President already gave me the okay! One more thing. It's been revealed that your friend and business partner is also a climbing buddy of yours."

"Yes, Tarkan Kirni," said Daniel. "We were supposed to go on a climb in the Alps this month but, uh, we had to postpone for business reasons, and then, the hijacking took over both our schedules, so we've decided to wait until next year. It's too bad. Both of us had whipped ourselves into shape for the climb."

"Hmm," mused the Secretary. "Have the doctors mentioned when they think your arm might heal?"

"Both gunshot wounds were superficial. They think I'll be back to normal in a week, provided I keep up the exercise routines they've prescribed. Why? Was there something you needed me to do now?"

"Where were you thinking of climbing?"

"We planned on climbing the Matterhorn, near Zermatt, Switzerland. It's something I've always wanted to do since I was a little boy. Here's a picture of it taken from the village. It's quite imposing, but we were planning on using the guide service."

The Secretary paused for a moment, taking the photo from Daniel. "Do you mind if I scan this in and send it to our security agents? Oh, and in case the President didn't tell you, we've arranged for a small security team to accompany you and your close friends and relatives for the next year. Hope you're okay with that."

"Yes" said Daniel. "And you can keep that if you like."

"What if you and your business partner were able to go through with the climb, say toward the end of the month?" she asked. "We could help make all of the arrangements— air, hotel, and all. And we'll even make the necessary connections for you with the guide service. Of course these arrangements would be fully at the expense of the U.S. government, and a security team would be with you even during the climb."

Daniel was surprised. "Yes, I would be all for it and I'm sure Tarkan would be as well. We sure would appreciate the assistance. Is there something else I should know about?"

"Yes. If the two of you were to do this together there would be quite a bit of publicity surrounding it, a lot in Turkey. But this would be a big boost for U.S.-Turkey relations. We would coordinate our diplomatic moves with the Turks, playing up both sides as supportive of the venture. If you're up for it, the implications for cooperation between our two countries would be enormous. Joint business ventures would become highly desirable. There are many positive implications."

"I never thought of it that way, Madam Secretary. I'd be glad to participate. I'm sure Tarkan would be too."

"I'll have our embassy make the necessary inquiries with him, involving the Turkish government every step of the way, of course. I will have to ask one more thing of you, though."

"What's that?"

"I'd like you to remain incommunicado with the outside world until the actual climb is finished, even with close friends in Seattle. That's why we have a security team arranged for you. There might still be angry Chechen-Georgian terrorist groups trying to get revenge. You can see the implications, right? And we'll make sure the press is able to cover it. They'll likely try to send live photos or videos to their editors when you've completed the climb."

"Yes, of course," responded Daniel. "I'll stay here for another day or so, then fly to Switzerland where I'll meet up with Tarkan. But I was hoping to communicate with friends and employees back in Seattle."

"Yes, I know you may have people you want to speak with, but my security folks are pretty experienced in these matters, and they are recommending we play this one cool for now. No contacts until the day the climb is finished. That includes texting and email. Your safety is still at risk. However, is there someone special to you that we can contact for you?

"Do you have a significant other? Someone else we should cover with a security detail? I'm only asking because if it became public knowledge their lives might be at risk as well."

"Well, there is my close friend, Arianna. And I was advised by Russian military officers our lives may be in danger of reprisals from the terrorist organization, so I'm worried about her safety. And my staff in Seattle."

"Yes, that is correct and we have several detailed procedures we would like you to follow. We'll go over those shortly. We'll contact these people for you.

"You are the number one public figure on people's minds right now. I hope you are comfortable with that."

"Yes...ahh, I don't see it as a problem."

"And terrorists! If there are more of them connected to the hijacking event, they would be an even bigger issue. So that's why I inquired about your friend, Arianna. Even though nothing may be happening right now, anything could develop in the future, and we just wanted to be sure you were aware of the risks to you and her of you being a high visibility figure. I hope you don't mind that we've done some background checking before the President asked you to join him in those programs. It's just the way things are done nowadays."

"I understand and I don't mind. I don't have anything to hide. I would consider it an honor to help you and the President. Ahh…you mentioned there was another objective I might help with?"

"Oh, yes. I believe the Russians have become even more enamored of you than the Turks, you having prevented a disaster at the Volgograd refineries and all. Putin will want you to go to Moscow for 'ceremonies'. The Russians are big on that. There are several things on our agenda with the Russians, and I think you have given us a good excuse to take the initiative.

"But, we need more time to sketch these things out. Let's stay focused on the Turks for now. Speaking of focus, we're late for lunch with Alan! We'd better be going!"

CHAPTER 13

Pursuit

Washington, D.C.
August 17, 2008

Arianna took the Metro from Reagan International Airport to DuPont Circle. Dragging her roll-aboard luggage behind her, she walked the six blocks to the Marriott Hotel recommended to her by Joan. As she checked in she felt the buzz of her cell phone. Glancing at the incoming number she pressed 'delete' and returned the phone to her pocket. "Don't know anyone from that number," she said to herself, although it was from a 202 area code, Washington, DC.

She headed to her room, still a little drowsy from the long flight.

The next day, she thought, "Right. Now how was I going to find Daniel? I'll try the State Department first. They should know." Most of the buildings at State were only a few blocks' walk from her hotel, so she headed south from DuPont Circle, finally approaching a DOS gate with security guards.

"Excuse me. I'm trying to find my friend, Daniel Prescott. He should have arrived here a day or two ago. He was the guy who saved everyone on that hijacked airliner in Russia. Do you know if I can find him here at the State Department?"

Completely taken by surprise at this brazen beauty making such a wild request, the security guards, one man, one woman, were a little slow to react. "Sorry, ma'am," said the male guard. "Who was it you were looking for?" The female guard, Christine Jacobs, a little faster in the 'heads-up' function looked a little more engaged and asked, "Is he an employee, ma'am?".

"Ah, no. He should have just arrived here maybe yesterday from Russia. He was the one who rescued all those folks from the hijacked airliner in Russia. He's a close friend of mine from Seattle and I was hoping to see him, even if just for a few minutes."

Agent Jacobs remembered the arrival of Daniel Prescott just four days ago under tight security and his visit to State for several hours with top diplomatic officials. The entire Department security force was put on high-alert status and advised to remain at that level for the next 48 hours.

Key words triggering her alarm bells were 'hijacked airliner' and 'Russia'. But she coolly proceeded with the next protocol steps to handle a possible security threat. "Ah, yes, ma'am. We'll do our best to find him. I just need a little more information. Would you come with me for a few minutes?" In a low voice she added to the male guard, "Jimmy, initiate a number seventeen, will you? Thanks."

Jacobs was a cute, spunky, but very serious security agent who had been with State almost nine years. She'd been fortunate enough to have been on a couple of overseas trips as part of the Secretary's visiting security team, having impressed her superiors with her good memory, high degree of technical and weapons savvy, fast learning capabilities, and, most importantly, her emotional intelligence. She gently led Arianna to a room nearby.

"This should be a good place to talk. Please, have a seat," she gestured. As Arianna made herself comfortable, Jacobs continued, "Sorry for the delay, ma'am, but we're advised to be pretty courteous and thorough in handling inquiring visitors. I'm sure you can understand. Especially with recent events regarding your friend, Mr. Prescott."

"Yes, of course," said Arianna. "He's a very close friend of mine, and when I heard he was returning to Washington, I immediately wanted to welcome him home. I'm from the other Washington—Seattle, that is," she added sheepishly.

"Sure, I understand perfectly," said Jacobs. "Now I've had my counterpart initiate a routine tracking protocol for Daniel. We'd just like to verify a few things along with our search. You wouldn't believe the number of crazies we get, claiming they personally know the Secretary, or one of her staff, things like that. We just have to be cautious. What did you say your full name was?"

"Arianna. Arianna Reynolds. I'm from Seattle and I've been a close friend of Daniel's for over three years."

"Yes, of course. Would you mind giving me your address, some ID and some contact information?"

"Yes. Here's my driver's license, and my cell and work phone are on this business card."

Arianna relaxed somewhat, then Jacobs then said, "Please wait here. I'll be a few minutes."

A half hour later Jacobs returned. "Well, we certainly appreciate you coming to Washington, giving Arianna back her driver's license. He did return from overseas, but I'm afraid that's all I can tell you, other than that he's no longer here."

Arianna became alarmed that she wouldn't be able to connect with Daniel. "Do you know where he went? Is he still in Washington? I really must find him. We're very close, you know. I just have to find him I came all this way. Even for just a few minutes…" Tears begin to well up in her eyes. Jacobs was empathetic but continued to be firm, following protocol.

"I'm sorry Miss Reynolds.. There's nothing more I can tell you…"

Jacobs knew she must continue to maintain protocol and her own emotions. But there was sincerity in Arianna's requests. "There might be one last chance," she thought. "I know I could get fired for this, but…" she reached out to touch Arianna's arm.

"Miss Reynolds, I realize he is a close friend. And we all admire what he did for those passengers on the aircraft just a few of days ago. It was a dramatic and brave thing he did. Ahh … Please excuse me for another few minutes."

Arianna nodded understanding, her red eyes showing the strain of giving up buckets of tears. She was able to contain her sobs as agent Jacobs departed once more.

Jacobs strode to the nearest vacant office and closed the door. She grabbed the phone and dialed an internal extension. "Get me Gloria Swanson in the Secretary's office.

Tell her this is Agent Jacobs in security. I need to talk with her right away." Jacobs hoped the Secretary's primary administrative assistant would remember her from the few times they worked together on the Secretary's international logistics planning team. "She can reach me at 2403. Yes, thank you."

"This is a long shot," thought Jacobs. "But I do know Daniel Prescott was here four days ago with the Secretary for a couple of hours. In that amount of time the two of them just might have mentioned his friends in Seattle. The Secretary has a lot of things going on every minute…Gloria will be doing me a big favor…I don't know why I'm sticking my neck out…It's just this woman seems so sincere.

"And if she actually is Prescott's close friend, then I know the Secretary would want to offer some comfort to her, even though she can't violate security protocols we've set up around his whereabouts. There's just a chance…"

Rrrrrring! The phone next to Jacobs came alive. "Security, Christine Jacobs," she answered.

"Christine! It's Gloria. I got your message. What's up?"

Agent Jacobs advised the primary office assistant of the Secretary of State about the visitor at the west gate. After a few minutes Jacobs said, "Yes, yes. I'll hold on." Her mind raced. Wow. I think Gloria's actually going to ask the Secretary right now. Oh, shit. I could really be in for it. I'll look like I cave in to any tourist who shows up looking for a connection… And then, when Gloria came back on: "What? What's that? Four-fifteen? Yes. I'll tell her. Thanks a million, Gloria. I owe you one."

"Wow," exclaimed Jacobs to herself. "That was fast! Really fast! Looks like the Secretary knows all about this woman! Okay. Here goes." Jacobs returned to where Arianna was waiting.

Before she could say anything, Arianna jumped up and began to apologize for her recent behavior. "I'm sorry I wasn't very objective. I really wanted to see Daniel so badly…"

"I fully understand, Miss Reynolds," said Jacobs, continuing to maintain a high degree of professionalism. "Please sit down. I do have something more to tell you."

Arianna, grateful for more news, waited for Jacobs to continue.

"As I said before, we know Daniel is not here. I know that must be disturbing for you but because of his status following the hijacking event we've had to implement high-security procedures regarding inquiries on his whereabouts." When Arianna's face fell again, Jacobs hurried on, "He has become a very important public figure now, and his security must be protected almost as much as the President's."

Hearing this, Arianna's mood changed from sadness to intrigue, as she began to understand the events surrounding the hijacking may have changed much about his freedom of movement.

"Miss Reynolds, we have verified who you are, and we are pleased to be of assistance to you as someone who has been a close friend of his. The Secretary of State has recently met with Mr. Prescott and would like to see you in her office. Just you, alone, today."

Arianna was stunned. "Oh,…I didn't realize what a big deal…"

"It *is* a big deal," said Jacobs, still retaining her no-nonsense demeanor. "This almost never happens. We usually have to shoo people away who make requests like yours. The Secretary would like to see you at four-fifteen this afternoon, if that's convenient with your schedule."

"Why, Yes…yes…ahh…I would be grateful for a chance to meet her and get news of Daniel," said Arianna.

"Well, because of security protocols, she may not be able to tell you much more than I have already. "And one more thing. We ask that you not discuss the Secretary's conversation, or our conversation, with anyone. This is for your security as well as Mr. Prescott's."

"Thank you, Agent Jacobs," said Arianna, when she had been escorted back to the entrance and returned her badge. "I'll be back here at four."

"Great. And please return to this gate and ask for me," handing Arianna her business card.

"I will. Thank you for all of your efforts," replied Arianna. She turned and exited the building at the west gate, feeling elated. "At least they know who I am now," she thought. "Hopefully they will eventually lead me to Daniel."

At five after four Arianna dutifully arrived back at the State Department West Entrance and asked for Agent Jacobs.

"You're right on time," said Jacobs, giving her another welcoming handshake. "Here is your new visitor badge. Just for your information, the solid blue color indicates a high level VIP."

They entered an elevator and Jacobs slid her security ID badge into the slot and punched '3'. The door opened and Jacobs said in a low voice, "Here we go." She led the way across the large reception area, stopping in front of Gloria Swanson's desk. Before she could identify her guest, the official-looking woman behind the desk rose and shook Jacobs' hand.

"Christine! Nice to see you again," said Swanson in a warm, welcoming voice. "And you must be Arianna Reynolds. How very nice to meet you. I'm Gloria Swanson."

Arianna, disarmed by this very professional and pleasant-looking woman, replied, "Nice to meet you, Ms. Swanson."

"The Secretary has been expecting you. And I understand you've come all the way from Seattle. I hope you've found some good accommodations in D.C."

As Swanson moved to accompany Arianna the next few steps to the Secretary's office, she eyeballed the extension lights on her phone console, confirming the Secretary of State was not on a call.

Jacobs separated herself from Arianna. "I'll be waiting out here for you. See you soon."

"Thank you, Agent Jacobs."

Swanson knocked, then opened the imposing oak-paneled door to the Secretary's office. "Arianna Reynolds to see you, Madam Secretary."

"Oh, yes. Bring her right in. How nice to see you. I've heard quite a bit about you already," the Secretary of State said in greeting, totally startling Arianna. "Oh, don't worry. They were all nice things. Thank you, Gloria." They shook hands cordially and the Secretary gestured to a comfortable set of chairs and sofa just to the side of her imposing desk.

"Do sit down. Well, your friend Daniel is quite a guy!" the Secretary began. "Everybody would like to see him. He's on everyone's list of 'Gotta see'!" she chuckled.

"Yes, I can imagine," Arianna declared, warming up to the Secretary's informal and friendly style. "I came here trying to find him myself. I've been a close friend of his for several years. I ... ahh... heard about the hijacking on the news and...ahh...just wanted to be there when he landed, even if it was the other Washington." Arianna managed a big grin.

"Yes, yes! And your instincts were well-founded. It had to be a very traumatic thing, fighting those terrorists, landing that plane, and all." The Secretary ran a mental checklist of what had already been on the news, a synopsis of which had been presented by her very capable staff four days ago.

"Ms. Reynolds, I would like to talk with you about a security issue, if you don't mind."

"Why, Yes, of course," gushed the beautiful woman from Seattle, thinking she was fortunate just to shake hands with this powerful icon of diplomacy.

"I just spoke with Daniel a few days ago," the Secretary began, noting Arianna's increased attentiveness. "As Agent Jacobs may have told you, there has been a high-security shield placed around him. He's now a major international figure and a huge asset to our country. We cannot disclose his whereabouts, even to relatives or close friends. Nor is he allowed to make or receive any phone calls, tweets, texts, or email messages, at least not for the next couple of weeks. By the way, did you receive a phone call from our office yesterday?"

"Oh, I ahh…don't think…" Then, remembering a 202 area code call that she didn't answer, she said, sheepishly, "I might have received one but I didn't talk to anybody."

"No matter. I can tell you now that we have our own security agents and I hope you'll accept the ones we've chosen for you. We plan to have a network of security people who will know your whereabouts at all times, even though its likely you won't notice them. They may contact you if you appear to be in any difficulty, wherever you may be."

"Oh, I see," said a surprised Arianna.

"Daniel told us you were a very important friend of his. We'd like to keep it that way. We suspect the terrorists Daniel defeated may find a way of getting revenge by harming you. Our security is designed to prevent that.

"I'm sorry to say I can't tell you much more than we've already discussed"

Arianna relaxed slightly, but was amazed she was getting security protection.

"Tell me, do you see Daniel often?"

"Yes, he's a wonderful guy. I…guess I've just been so busy at work and all. We do things together a couple of times a week," she smiled.

The Secretary paused for several seconds. "Well, you two have been together awhile, and it sounds like you get along wonderfully. Well, I hope something does work out for both of you."

Arianna sensed their conversation was about to wrap up but was surprised when the Secretary made a final comment.

"Ms. Reynolds, its been a pleasure meeting you." As she rose to end the meeting, she walked toward her desk, where she paused in front of her computer screen and placed her hand on the top of the display.

"I actually would be violating security protocols if I told you where he was, and, of course I couldn't do that. After all, I wrote the protocols!" The Secretary smiled as she hit several keys on her computer. But in the same instant she uttered those words, her hand flipped the monitor around, revealing a full screen photograph viewable from Arianna's chair.

Arianna uttered a "*GASP*," then covered her mouth, her eyes growing wide. There, on the screen, was a duplicate image of the photo Daniel gave her just a few days ago, the Swiss village of Zermatt, with the famous snow-covered Matterhorn!

It took her a few seconds to comprehend. "The Secretary was trying to tell me something." Arianna thought, "No, since she can't *tell* me, she's trying to *show* me! My God. That's where Daniel must be!"

"And now, my dear, I hope you have a pleasant visit for the rest of the time you're in Washington," said the Secretary of State as she extended her hand. She handed Arianna her business card. "Please reach me at this contact information if you need to talk to me for whatever reason. There's a security code included that means you're a special caller. It may take awhile but I'll try my best to get back to you."

Arianna took the Secretary's hand in both of hers, her heart pumping with excitement,"Good-bye. I can't thank you enough."

The Secretary opened the door to her office and discovered Agent Jacobs sitting in the waiting area. The rest of the staff was gone for the day. "Oh, Christine, would you escort Ms. Reynolds, please? And would you drop by my office when you're done? There's something I wanted to share with you."

"Absolutely. Thank you, Madam Secretary."

"Thank you again, Madam Secretary," said Arianna as she returned a wave good-bye.

Jacobs and Arianna entered the elevator and a few more seconds of silence followed as the elevator reached the ground floor. "Miss Reynolds, do you realize you had an audience with the Secretary of State for a full thirty minutes? I mean, it must have been something important. And, she called me 'Christine'! Can you believe that? That never happens. Never. It must mean she likes me or I screwed up, big time. And why would she call me back to her office when no one else is there? Oh, no! I really like this job. Been doing it for nine years. I just don't know…"

"I'll bet it's going to be something good," said Arianna, affectionately.

"Thank you for believing in me and taking the initiative to get me an audience with the Secretary. I look forward to seeing you again, sooner than later, I hope," stopping to shake hands.

"Good-bye and good luck on your search," Jacobs said with a wave good-bye.

Arianna returned the gesture as she headed out the door and turned up 21st Street NW, which was crowded with rush-hour traffic. "I'd better see about getting a booking on a flight to Switzerland tomorrow. I'll probably have to fly into Geneva and then take a train," she told herself as she glanced back at the State Department complex, where the third floor lights were still on.

The Secretary of State welcomed Agent Jacobs back to her office to congratulate her for showing, tact, initiative and attention to proper protocol when handling a sensitive and highly-important visitor.

"After all," the Secretary reminded herself, when Jacobs had gone again, "Situations like this are not standard operating procedure. This kind of initiative must be rewarded and encouraged. It's about time for Jacobs to get some more training and enter the ranks of management," she mused, as she reached for her phone to make an important international call on another matter...

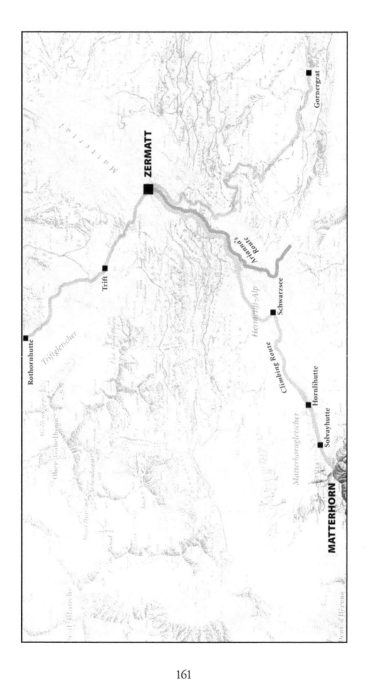

Gornergrat

ZERMATT

Matter[...]

Arnold's Summit Route

Trift

Trift[...]

Rothornhutte

Schwarzsee

Hernetti-Alp

Climbing Route

Hornlihutte

Solvayhutte

Matterhorngletscher

MATTERHORN

9

CHAPTER 14
Zermatt

~~~~~~

Visp, Switzerland   651 meters   2,136 feet
August 17, 2008

Daniel gazed out the window of the red train of the Matterhorn-Gotthard-Bahn railway on its journey from the town of Visp, Switzerland, south along the Mattervispa River. The trip from Visp, at 651 meters altitude, to Zermatt at 1,606 meters, took approximately an hour and twenty minutes. Daniel divided his time between gazing at the mountain-rich scenery, discussions with three State Department security escorts, and thoughts of Arianna. He wondered if she heard about the hijacking and, if so, how she reacted.

"Well, Daniel," asked Tom Renshaw, "Ready to grab some altitude?" The three agents accompanied him at the request of the Secretary of State and would climb with him and continue their protective presence through their planned visit to Istanbul, following the climb. Renshaw, the lead security agent, was joined by agents Steve Thompson, and Joseph Appleton. All were seasoned, professional security experts, in addition to being excellent climbers. Renshaw had even climbed in the Zermatt area two years earlier and made arrangements for the party's climb and hotel accommodations.

"I'm ready. The arm is okay and I haven't stopped daily workouts since Rostov."

"Good," said Renshaw. Now you can maximize the acclimatization benefits before the climb."

"Lets do it," exhulted Daniel. "Looks like we have a pretty heavy schedule afterward."

"You bet."

Tarkan, who would be joining them in Zermatt, would also accompany Daniel and the security men to Istanbul, following the climb. The Secretary of State's agenda for publicity and business connections would be the main event on their return to Istanbul.

"I hear your business partner is bringing along a new climbing buddy, Mustafa. Initial reports say he's an excellent climber. How's his English?"

"Tarkan's is excellent. Don't know about Mustafa. We'll find out tonight at dinner."

"All events in Istanbul are scheduled for after Ramadan, the Muslim holy month, just so there are no conflicts with local sentiment," added Renshaw.

The train continued to follow the Mattervispa River south and entered the awesome, forty kilometer-long Mattertal, a steep-sided valley. Along the way it passed dozens of beautiful side valleys, each of which led to one or more glaciers at the base of the most spectacular collection of alpine peaks in Europe, a climber's paradise.

"Isn't this fabulous?" noted Renshaw. "You could spend an entire summer in this area and be hard pressed to climb all of the 4,000-meter giants of the Mattertal, Saastal, Val d' Zinal, and Val d' Herrens, where the German part of Switzerland meets it's French counterpart."

The technically-efficient Swiss had completed several cable car routes up the mountainsides from the railway, allowing tiny alpine villages to flourish as tourist meccas clinging precariously to the sides of the spectacular valleys.

For hundreds of years the Mattertal was just a sleepy valley with small farms, tiny villages, and dirt roads and trails as the only routes of passage. It remained obscure until 1865, when Edward Whymper, an early British mountaineer, made the first ascent of the Matterhorn. One hundred and thirty years later the valley boasted a railway up its entire length, a private road, and resort villages like Zermatt, which generated a tidy amount of tourism income.

As the story of the famous Matterhorn spread, so did the number of visitors to Zermatt, growing from 12,000 per year in Whymper's day to well over 300,000 per year in 2007. Many came in winter, attracted by dozens of cable lifts and ski runs clustered around the area.

By mid-afternoon the train reached the Zermatt Bahnhof, or train station. Daniel and the agents retrieved their luggage and packs from the overhead rack and made their way out to the massive platform, where a dozen porters in small electric carts waited for tourists.

"Don't worry, guys. I've got this all arranged. See, there's our porter, Henri, waiting to take us to our hotel.

Daniel wasn't paying attention, completely awestruck by his first view of the fearsome-looking Matterhorn. "Uhh, I think its gonna take more than a couple of practice climbs to do THAT thing."

Recent rains in the village had brought fresh snow to the steep giant that jutted 4,478 meters, or 14,691 feet into the sky. Daniel was overwhelmed. This was nothing like other mountains he'd summited.

Tom Renshaw overheard him and tried to steady his charge, "We'll be fine. We're climbing with expert guides that know the safest routes. Not to worry. Piece of cake!"

Daniel could only continue to stare at the huge, white pyramid.

"C'mon," urged Tom. "Let's get to the hotel, stow our gear and get some dinner. We can do more technical talk when we go over the route with the guides."

Daniel complied but was clearly shaken by the sheer enormity of task presented by the imposing mountain. It sure looked a lot steeper than the pictures he'd seen.

With their gear secured in their rooms, the three agents and Daniel took the short walk to the Zermatt Führerverein, or bureau for climbing guides. They discovered, through prior arrangements, the chief guide had already assigned four guides to the team. These men were chosen for their previous experience with U.S. security agents, either on climbs or by moonlighting as local contractors for U.S. security personnel accompanying American VIPs. As they exited the bureau, Daniel noted, with wonder, the large brass statue of an ibex guarding the front entrance, the symbol of alpine agility.

"Sure would like to have that statue in our office reception area," he mused, thinking of his company's logo.

As they made their way to a restaurant on the Bahnhofstrasse, Daniel realized, "Sure seems awfully quiet for a town with so many tourists."

"That's because there aren't any cars," said Tom, smiling. "Much of the transportation is done by electric carts. And nearly everyone walks to their destination. No hydrocarbon pollution in this town."

Renshaw chose this particular restaurant for reasons similar to the choice of hotel. The cuisine was excellent, but the clientele were generally European outdoor types, not ostentatious businessmen. Again, low-key being the byword.

Prior to dinner, the four Americans settled into a reserved section of the hotel's well-stocked bar. As they completed their first round of beers, Daniel sensed someone close behind him.

Before he could turn around, a voice bellowed, "I thought they didn't allow Americans in this bar!" Daniel spun around and was greeted with a bear hug from Tarkan. He was accompanied by Mustafa, his recent climbing partner.

"My fellow Americans, please meet my climbing partner, Mustafa." Tarkan used a joking reference to the manner of speaking used by Nixon almost forty years ago, and, as always, tried to emulate American colloquialisms to fit in with the Yankee crowd. The Americans would have ample opportunity to have fun with Tarkan's attempted U.S. slang, an important bonding practice and all in good fun.

Laughter resounded as Daniel introduced Tarkan and Mustafa to Tom Renshaw and the U.S. security detail. Daniel watched Mustafa closely for a few minutes. The man possessed a solid build, strong arms and legs, and, of course, the requisite mustache common to most Turkish men.

But he noted Mustafa didn't mix socially as well as Tarkan. Daniel thought, "Maybe it was because his business partner was so gregarious."

He reminded himself Tarkan does not take easily to boasting or insincere men. Mustafa must have been well-vetted by Tarkan for this security assignment, even though his English was rudimentary.

Just then, a buxom Fräulein who was their server brought another round of liter mugs filled with golden-foamed Swiss beer, and, as she departed, Tarkan said, *"Allah, Allah.* Oh, My God," causing the other men to smile. "We have those in Turkey also." The smiles turned into bigger grins. *"Karpus.* Watermelons!" declared Tarkan.

Long peals of laughter rang through the room. Daniel joined in, still smiling when it had died down.

The attractive woman who was their server understood English perfectly and, as she returned to the kitchen, with a smile and a blush said, *"Dummkopf Americanisher Scheiss,"* Stupid American Shit, the men at the table still laughing at Tarkan's comments.

A few beers and a filling dinner later, they all retired to the hotel as they would start early the next day. The first of three rugged acclimatizing hikes to boost their ability to perform at higher altitude began at 0830 hours.

The men were up with an early dawn and, after a solid continental breakfast of sausage, black bread, fruit, yogurt, and coffee, they grabbed the ample bag lunches prepared by the kitchen staff.

"Gentlemen," Renshaw announced as breakfast was winding down. "Our objective of the day: the Rothornhütte, at 3,198 meters, an elevation gain of 1,592 meters, or 5,223 feet! This hefty day's workout was recommended by the Führerverein for the first day of acclimatization. Not to worry, guys. A walk in the park!"

It would let the men know early whether or not they were in proper shape to take on a more challenging climb and would allow them to ratchet down their training climbs as they approached their main event in another three days.

Daniel's wounds had all but completely healed, and he experienced minimal difficulty carrying his pack as the men hit the trail along the Triftbach valley, ascending in a northwesterly direction from the main part of Zermatt. The weather was clear and the temperature about 50F. After a kilometer Daniel hung back and settled in with a pace to match Tarkan's.

"So, Tarkan, what happened in Istanbul when everyone learned of the hijacking?" he asked his friend.

"Everybody freak out," Tarkan answered. "No one expect it, even with war in Georgia. No one could tell plane was hijacked until it in Russia and the terrorists make mistake of executing captain. Those bastards were crazy. And they would have killed all passengers, including me and thirty other Turks, my countrymen, if it weren't for you."

Daniel countered, "Well, don't forget I had plenty of help, Bill, Matt, and that ATC from Novorossiysk…"

"Daniel, remember, without you taking big risk first, everyone die!"

Tarkan continued, "As soon as they heard airplane was safe in Russia, everyone in Istanbul went crazy. People hug each other in streets. A huge crowd formed in Tadzik Square and Prime Minister Erdogan came out to speak. It was ballistic, yes?

"Turkish, American, and Russian flags all over. Daniel, you did real good. Turkish, people wait for you. They go crazy when you come back to Istanbul."

Daniel listened as his friend continued for a while about the Turkish reaction to the hijacking and safe return of all the passengers and Daniel related the story behind his empowering dream.

"It must have been the image of the snow leopard on that carpet in your friend's shop in Istanbul," he said. "Maybe it was the stress of the hijacking, but my mind created a fantasy around that mysterious animal.

"In my dream, when it hit the rocks it made a loud noise, and I woke up. And then I clearly saw if I was ever going to see Arianna again, I would have to put aside all my fears of being harmed by the hijackers and take the fight to them, no matter what."

Tarkan was speechless for a few moments, then let out a low whistle, "*Whew*. Good thing ibex win battle and Daniel become Macho Man or we all dead from snow leopard!"

They hiked on for a while, trading banter about business and the failed attempt at gaining more credit.

Continuing along the Triftbach, the creek fed by the massive Triftgletscher, they reached the halfway point to the Rothornhütte, and time for lunch.

Daniel and Tarkan were separated by a small distance from the rest of the party and, as they munched on black bread, cheese, and fruit.

Tarkan asked him, "Hey, man. You spend the rest of your life like the ibex, hop from ledge to ledge? Always fight predators or weather? When you settle down, man? You know, even ibex need good home life with lady ibex and little ones to protect. They give you purpose different from conflict with snow leopard. You know that friend of yours, Arianna. She nice lady. What about her?"

"Yeah," replied Daniel. "She's a terrific lady. I've known her three years now. We've done so much together. I've tried several times to get her interested in talking about being more serious but she just doesn't seem interested. We're just friends in her mind, even though I have really strong romantic feelings for her."

"Daniel. Don't be such *tavuk bok*, chickensheet!" Tarkan exclaimed. "When you gonna get balls, man? I mean tell her. She class lady. When you gonna get another one like her? I've known you for five years, man, you used to be timid. But you different now, more confident and solid. Maybe it was hijacking. Anyway, go ahead. Kick ass! Just tell her."

Just then Tom Renshaw came over to see how Daniel and Tarkan were faring. "You guys okay?" he inquired. Both men nodded in response and waited for Tom to wander away again.

"Yes, Tarkan, yes," sighed Daniel. "Agreed. But American women are different now. You can't just go in there like a cave man and, '*bonk*', claim your woman! Most women are more tied up in their careers than ever before. It's harder. It's like they have a different radar. They're taking much longer to get married, and even longer to have kids. And, they're becoming much better educated than men," Daniel said, sounding exasperated now. "You know, love takes time."

"***Boktan***. Bullsheet! You Americans make too freakin' complicated! Your babies must be delivered by storks! You don't have time for sex! Just tell her you love her. True isn't it?"

"Why, yes, of course."

"Then do it. You want to go through rest of life alone? Like ibex? Like snow leopard? Love her and make family. I don't want business partner who is alone. He is pain in ass!"

A few moments of silence passed. Daniel knew Tarkan had a point. He had been attracted to Arianna for several years. They've gotten along so well, and even had disagreements that were quickly resolved.

"Have I been a big wimp? he wondered. "What if Tarkan is right? I've gotta be more aggressive and tell her my feelings."

He recognized she had dreams of her own and her own agenda. He wanted to talk more about these things with her, but they needed to be discussed face to face.

"But with all the diplomatic traveling that's been scheduled for me I might not even get home for another month or two!" he sighed.

Rothornhütte   3,198 meters   10,492 feet
August 18, 2008

The group continued its ascent of the valley and came within sight of the Gablehorngletscher, then the even more massive Triftgletscher, as they reached a rest stop at 2,579 meters, about three kilometers distance from the Rothornhütte.

Such massive displays of permanent ice attested to the power of altitude in the Alps. Much of the moisture moving north from the Mediterranean Sea had been trapped by this 3,000 – 4,000 meter barrier, a process that had continued for millenia.

Finally they spied the Hütte, just another 270 meters upward along a multi switch-back trail. At 1430 hours they reached the gray stone, two-story structure with heavy shutters flanking each window. In characteristically Swiss fashion, the shutters were painted red and white, both a reflection of the Swiss national colors as well as for safety. Such colors were prominent in assisting climbers locating it in white-out conditions.

Surrounding the Hütte on two sides was a strong, chain-link fence serving as a deflector shield for stray rocks cascading from above and acting as an avalanche fence in winter.

All five men collapsed in front of the Hütte, not just a shelter, but a full-fledged overnight oasis for climbers, complete with bunk beds and hearty meals to sustain an average burn of 4,000 calories per day. In typical Swiss fashion, it served as a base for those attempting the nearby summits of at least six mountains, all over four thousand meters.

The men donned their down vests and rain jackets and moved outside to sit on comfortable benches overlooking the Trifthorn and Triftgletscher to the west. Daniel took in the spectacular view, still breathing rapidly due to the thin air. To the northeast was the ridge marking the southern extent of the Rothorngletscher.

Nine kilometers to the south was the tip of the Matterhorn, at 4,478 meters, almost daring Daniel to begin the ascent that day. "Easy now. Plenty of time to get there. And I'll be stronger after these training climbs," he mused.

The Hütte was positioned on large rock shelf at nearly 3,200 meters, with a 210-degree view, a lofty end to that day's 1,600 meter elevation gain.

They were exhausted, and, thanks to Tom Renshaw's foresight, would be spending the night there, gaining valuable high-altitude acclimatization time in the process. The Rothornhütte was one of hundreds of such facilities of the SAC chain, or Swiss Alpine Club. Their rustic overnight accommodations allowed climbers to conquer multiple summits and keep a Hütte as a base camp. Tom had learned of this invaluable network of Hütten during his climbing adventures two years ago.

He had made reservations for the team via his connections at the Führerverein in Zermatt, as soon as he was alerted by the State Department of Daniel's and Tarkan's plans. Tom and the other two agents joined Daniel and Tarkan on the deck and each brought a liter of fresh water, a hefty buttered biscuit, and half a bar of Swiss chocolate.

"Good work, gentlemen," said Tom. "Tomorrow we descend to Zermatt and the hotel and take the rest of the day off. Any objections?"

"No way. Is good idea," grunted Tarkan, echoing Daniel's thoughts. "So glad we don't carry tents, sleeping bags, stoves, and food."

"The following day will be our second training climb," continued Tom. "That will be the Gornergrat, at 3,135 meters, almost as high as we are today. Then we rest one day. The next day we ascend to the Hörnlihütte, rest there one night, and make the final assault on the Matterhorn early the next morning. Eat up as much as you like tonight. I've arranged for extra grub if you need it."

Tarkan asked with an inquisitive look, "What is 'grub'?" The Americans responded with well-intended snickers. "You must have missed the episodes of *Bonanza, Rawhide*, and *The Good, the Bad, and the Ugly*," Steve Thompson exulted with a belly laugh. "Yeah, especially the Ugly," laughed Joseph Appleton. Tarkan gave a playful curse under his breath in Turkish, "**Bokumu ye**. Freakin' crazy guys," prompting another burst of laughter. Finally a call came from within the Hütte for dinnertime.

Daniel lingered a few more minutes as the others filed in to the dinner table. Gazing south at the Matterhorn, doubts again entered his mind. "Wow, that thing is steep. And it's still snow-covered, which means there's also snow and ice on the climbing route."

A strange quiet came over him as the first small cloud descended between his position and the Trifthorn. "This is where it could have been," he thought, reconstructing the encounter between the ibex and the snow leopard in his mind. Directly in his view, multiple ledges, snow chutes, and knife-like ridges all served as touch points of an imagined chase between the two animals. "Back and forth there, leaping over here," Daniel continued to replay the story in his mind, until, once more, the final **thud** of the snow leopard hitting the rocks below jolted him from his meditative state.

Time for grub and a warm woolen blanket.

Terminal de Genève Aéroport
Genève, Switzerland
August 19, 2008

Bing! Bang! Bong! The soft musical tones of the PA system rang in the Terminal de Genève Aéroport and a gate change announcement followed in French, German, and English. Thousands of other travelers scurried to and fro. It was August, and the European vacation season was in full swing. Arianna Reynolds, still a little woozy from the ten-hour flight from Washington, towed her roll-aboard behind her and shifted the load of her backpack to a more comfortable position.

She queued up to pass through immigration and customs, her wobbly legs reminding her of how little she was able to sleep on airplanes. "Oh, well. Maybe I'll get some shut-eye on the train," she hoped.

After passing through the Swiss *douane,* or customs, she checked in for directions at the Gare CFF Aeroport and was able to purchase a train ticket all the way to Zermatt via Lausanne and Martigny. It was a four-hour journey requiring one change of trains. But first she had to catch the light rail from the airport to downtown Genève and catch the 0936 train to Visp from the Gare Cornavin, Geneva's central train station.

"Arrghh," she groaned, "the timing is going to be really tight. It's already 0900 hours and the train to Zermatt departs at 0936 hours. And I don't know my way around, which means I'll need time to ask for directions in a city where everyone speaks French!"

To her surprise, Genève was a city where nearly everyone also spoke English, and she had little difficulty finding the connection to Gare Cornavin. But the train was delayed eight minutes en route to downtown, an eternity by Swiss standards, due to an accident on a construction site next to the train tracks. Highly unusual in precise, efficient Switzerland, but, Arianna realized, *stuff happens.*

She arrived at Cornavin at 0932 and bolted from the light-rail car. "Which way to the Geneve-Visp train?" She hurriedly asked for directions, sprinted across the crowded terminal and was just able to grab the ascending bar to the green and gold train as it began to draw away from the platform.

"Whoa, that was close" she said breathlessly, dropping herself into the nearest available seat in a 2nd *Classe* car.

By chance she ended up next to another slender, blonde female reading a *Let's Go!* travel book, dressed in a light jacket and jeans which had several fashionably-placed patches, all the rage with the younger set in most western countries. Pretty and energetic, she smiled at Arianna when their glances met. "Glad you made it."

Arianna recognized the accent as decidedly American, and responded, "Yeah. Didn't think I was going to. I'm Arianna."

"Amber," was the reply, as she shook Arianna's hand. "Been traveling long?"

"Just got here. I'm on my way to Zermatt to…ahh…hopefully meet a friend. You look like you've been traveling a while."

"Yeah," Amber laughed. "You could say that. Just came from southern France and heading to Munich to see a friend."

Arianna was impressed with her reply and apparent worldliness. "Probably speaks fluent French and can find her way most anywhere," Arianna thought. "Looks like she's in her mid-thirties and has that carefree spirit about her. And she looked very 'hip'."

The two women talked, and, between the conversation and the breathtaking scenery along Lake Geneva, Arianna forgot her jet lag for the moment.

The backdrop of the Alps confirmed she was closing in on her destination. Arianna remembered she couldn't reveal much about her itinerary or her 'friend', for security reasons, so she listened attentively to Amber's tales of adventure in the south of France.

During the lapses in conversation, Arianna became pensive about her journey, still wondering if she hadn't overreacted about Daniel.

"He's somewhere in that rocky and icy splendor," she thought, staring out the window. "I only hope I can find him before he's off on another adventure, or taken captive by another government that wants him to give speeches, or, whatever."

Stops in Lausanne, Vevey, and Montreux afforded the opportunity to witness the contrast of compact European cities with the wildness of the Alps.

"These houses are all so neatly integrated. What marvelous planning and design."

"Yes, the architecture of Europe is timeless," observed Amber. "My four weeks in France were filled with so much eye-pleasing architecture, ingeniously designed into the landscape. Switzerland is very similar. You're going to enjoy your time here, I just know it."

Twenty minutes later Arianna observed, "Look at these mountains," as the train headed southeast into the canyons of the Swiss Alps, now rising to over 3,000 meters in altitude, just a few kilometers from the tracks. The rhythm of the railroad lulled her into a catnap, and she advised Amber of her desire to nod off for a few minutes.

Unknown to either woman their movements and conversation were monitored by an attentive, dark skinned, husky man three rows forward on the left side of the train. He expertly obscured himself from their view while still keeping them in earshot.

Arianna's jet lag extended her nap for the better part of an hour and she was awakened by Amber who reminded her about her designated stop at Visp.

"Oh, thank you for waking me. It's been so great visiting with you. I sure would like to stay in touch." She fumbled for a business card to hand to Amber.

"Here, I'll give you my email," said Amber, ripping off a page corner from her guidebook.

"Bye, and good luck." Arianna gave Amber a small hug and Amber responded with the European tradition of air kisses on each cheek.

"Amber must have picked that up in France. People sure are friendly here," she thought as she waved goodbye one more time then donned her backpack and towed her roll-aboard out to the platform at Visp.

At the same time, the dark man left the train from the forward exit, opposite Arianna, and skillfully concealed himself until bolting into the Visp Bahnhof, still keeping her in sight.

What the man didn't know or see was another man, dressed in hiking clothes, who was last to descend from the train and follow him into the station.

Visp, Switzerland   651 meters   2,136 feet
August 19, 2008
1230 hours

Arianna had completed three-quarters of her train journey, and had to wait eighteen minutes in Visp for the train to Zermatt.

As she sat on a bench on the Visp Bahnhof platform the dark skinned man observed her from inside the terminal.

"She is easy to follow," noted the rough-looking man. "I'll be looking forward to my second half payment of $100,000 from Anatoly in a few days. But this is not the location to make a move. Better to wait for another chance in Zermatt."

On the platform, Arianna grew skittish,, longing for her office routine in Seattle. Big houses with big lawns. Big freeways. Big grocery stores. Big cars. "And why am I taking the train? What if I can't find him? What if he's in the mountains and they won't tell me his whereabouts?

"I know Daniel has had a bigger interest in me. It was probably a romantic interest, but I never encouraged him. I always wanted it to be a safe friendship."

Just when it seemed she would turn and flee, Arianna thought, "Wait a minute. I've come all this way. Look at these beautiful mountains. They're an important part of Daniel's life. Shouldn't I learn to know them also? Besides, this is an adventure. Just look at how happy and calm Amber seemed. She's definitely doing something for herself…no… doing something to *discover* herself. And, I've already paid for my…"

Bing! Bang! Bong! The tones of the Bahnhof PA system chimed an impending announcement. Arianna waited for the English words: "Ladies and gentlemen. The 1248 train to Zermatt is departing on platform three. Please proceed to your train and have a pleasant trip."

The sight of the beautiful mountains and excitement of seeing Daniel sparked an adventurous mood and she boarded the train for a forty-kilometer ride up the magic Mattertal.

Just as the red train began its slow departure from the platform the dark man slipped into an adjacent car, having noted where Arianna was seated.

He was followed a few seconds later by another man who boarded at the back end of Arianna's car.

All three were now headed toward Zermatt where their paths were destined to cross!

Hörnlihütte   3,260 meters   10,695 feet
August 19, 2008
1430 hours

"Good workout, boys. Glad we were packin' light," said Tom Renshaw as he tossed his pack on the sun deck of the Hörnlihütte, the SAC mountain 'hut' where they would rest that night.

The Hütte, at 3,260 meters, was originally constructed in 1868, and was expanded and remodeled in 1890, 1915, and 1965. No mere 'hut' by American standards, it was a rough hotel with bunk beds, a large dining area, and a fully-outfitted kitchen, just like the Rothornhütte. Its use by climbers headed to the summit of the Matterhorn had proved essesntial as the mountain's popularity grew enormously over the past hundred years. The Hutte had saved the lives of many climbers during that period, as the unpredictability of weather and accidents gave rise to many emergencies.

"Those previous two training climbs did wonders. I'm barely feeling any effect of the altitude. Ready to go for the summit tomorrow?" Tom asked. He glanced toward Daniel and Tarkan. They had all just completed a 1,650 meter elevation gain from Zermatt.

"Yeah. No problem," answered Daniel. "I feel the same way. You really took us to task during the past four days but it's really paid off. Tarkan, what about you?"

"Yeah, yeah. Ready to bite ass off donkey," joked the Turk. "Just give me good grub tonight." He laughed and the others echoed his jollity.

It was early afternoon and they had made excellent time. They each gulped down a liter of water, a large chunk of dark, hearty bread smothered with Nussbutter, and the ubiquitous Swiss chocolate bar, all retrieved by Tom from inside the Hütte. Their packs had been kept intentionally light, with some of their extra clothing, ice axes, crampons, and food carried by Tom's security team. The intention was to have Daniel, Tarkan and Mustafa as rested as possible for the climb the next day.

"Remember, guys, tomorrow we're going to do an elevation gain of 1,218 meters, but jammed into one fifth as much distance. It's 4,000 vertical feet from here to the summit, but compressed into a horizontal distance of less than a mile. In other words, this will be the steepest scramble of your lives. Steep and relentless. So load as many carbs as you can today 'cause you'll be burning all of 'em off tomorrow."

"**Bok**. Holee sheet," exclaimed Tarkan. "So that's it." He spun around to eyeball the near-vertical route along the Hörnligrat, the knife edged ridge dividing the east and north faces of the mountain.

Daniel, who had been gazing down the valley at Zermatt and its surroundings, turned and surveyed the climbing route up the Matterhorn. Already, clouds were starting to cling to the north and east faces, acting as magnets to add more moisture to their growing mass.

"Hope the weather holds," he muttered. "We've come a long way. Am I glad this Hütte is here."

"Amen to that, Daniel," said Tom. "We'll have the best chance if we get an early start, so the guides will wake us at 0430 hours tomorrow morning."

"No way," groaned Tarkan. "We bust ass to get here just to wake at four-thirty?"

"That's why we brought headlamps for you," explained Tom. "Our first 45 minutes of climbing tomorrow morning will be in the dark!"

"You sheeting me?" gawked Tarkan. "We fall off cliff and break ass!"

"No, no," Tom reassured him. "It's done all the time. All these climbers do the same. Besides we have the best guides money can buy. They'll be leading the way."

"How you know guides are best?" inquired Tarkan.

"Because they're Swiss," said Tom. "And their training is second to none. They're constantly refreshing their skills every climbing season. They put in many hours of climbs before they even start taking on clients, each year. These guys are tough as nails. Of course, all bets are off if they get a cranky client like you."

"What?" said Tarkan, surprised.

"Maybe they'll just let you fall off the mountain if you give them too much bullsheeeet," Tom mimicked Tarkan's accent, causing the rest of the team to break out in howls of laughter. Tarkan knew he'd fallen victim to the Americans' jokes yet again. He grinned. "*Bokumu Ye.*" he said, prompting more laughter.

Daniel noticed other climbers beginning to assemble on the sun deck, and picked out conversations in German, French, Italian, and English. But he occasionally heard a language he couldn't identify. "Climbers from all over the world," he mused. This was a popular mountain. He was glad Tom could get them reservations for the Hütte and the guide service!

"I just checked with the guides inside," he said. "The weather is iffy for tomorrow. Could be good or not so good. Could go either way. Also, I'll be going with you, Tarkan and Mustafa tomorrow, while Steve and Joseph keep a sharp eye for us here at the Hörnlihütte. There's usually a lot of climbing traffic on this popular mountain, so we'll want to keep our party size to a minimum. Each one of us will be roped to a Swiss guide. If the weather holds, they'll get us up and back with no problems."

Zermatt   1,606 meters   5,269 feet
August 19, 2008
1345 hours

The train slowed at it approached the Zermatt Bahnhof. Arianna's anxiety was high. "What if I see him? Do I first say 'Hi, it's me. Just dropped in to see you'?"

"I don't think so." Then she reminded herself that it was she who was going through a lot of effort to see Daniel, not the other way around.

As she descended to the Bahnhof platform, she inhaled sharply. There, standing like a white sentinel over the village, was the Matterhorn, just like in Daniel's picture. "My God, how beautiful," she exclaimed to herself. After another a few seconds she added aloud, "Jeepers, the air is pretty thin here."

Behind her about ten meters away the dark skinned man descended to the platform and quickly walked in the other direction. As before, another man followed him from a safe distance.

Moments later a man on an electric cart called out, "Excuse me, Miss. Can I take you to a hotel?" Knowing she needed to get her bearings, Arianna asked, "Is there a climbing guide office or bureau?"

"Yes, Miss. The Führerverein. I can take you. No problem. It is close by." The cart bounced along the cobblestone streets and within three minutes halted in front of the climbing office.

Arianna dismounted and offered the man three francs. "Oh, no. You don't pay me. I'll wait here for you. When you come out I can take you to a hotel. Okay?"

Arianna, taken aback by this show of hospitality, managed a smile and replied, "*Danke.* I will check on some things then come back here."

There were several men standing outside the building who appeared to be extremely fit. "They must be guides," she thought. Just as she entered the Führerverein, she noticed one of the men exchanging a quick glance with the cart driver. "That's odd," she thought. "I wonder if they're know each other? After all, it is a small town. And no use trying to look glam! I don't want to stand out." She pulled out a dowdy-looking rain parka out of her pack.

Inside she found a semi-chaotic scene, with climbing types speaking and gesturing in a dozen different languages, packs and climbing gear of all shapes and sizes underfoot, and frenzied staff trying to locate reservations, schedules, and tariff contracts. "Seems normal," Arianna thought.

"After all, it's high season for climbing." She got in the shortest line and waited for ten minutes, surveying the huge variety of people and equipment, until finally a friendly voice from behind the counter said, "*Bitte, kann ich Ihnen helfen?*" Then instantly in English, "Hello, may I help you?"

"Yes, *danke*," replied Arianna. "I am looking for my friend. He was expected to do some climbing here and I wonder how I might contact him."

"What was his name?" the man asked.

"Prescott," replied Arianna. The man searched computer records for a few moments, then slowly said, "No, I don't see anyone by that name. Is he with a climbing party and would you know its name?"

Arianna grew worried. "Shit," she said to herself. "I was afraid this would happen. How am I supposed to find him if he's not registered here? I can't possibly inquire at 150 hotels!"

Despair crept into her voice, "This would be the only place I could think of to find him. I just don't have any other way of knowing…"

"I'm sorry, Miss. We don't have any record of someone with that name. Perhaps he is with a private climbing party. There are so many who come to climb the mountains in Zermatt. Did you know which mountain was his objective? There are dozens in this area. In some cases it might be possible…"

"The Matterhorn," Arianna hurriedly interjected. "He is supposed to be climbing the Matterhorn."

"In that case, I'm afraid I can't help you, Miss. There are hundreds attempting that climb, just in this week alone."

Her despair deepening, Arianna murmured, "Thank you. *Danke,*" turning away from the information counter looking down at the floor. She was out of options. She didn't have a clue how to proceed. She couldn't start a massive search for Daniel. His location was supposed to remain unknown, for security reasons. She couldn't contact the State Department. Even the tip from the Secretary was in confidence.

"I'm at the end of the road. I guess I'll just have to go home," she choked back the tears beginning to well up in her eyes. Her despair was accentuated by the frenzied activity in the Führerverein. Climbers and guides bustling to and fro. People speaking in strange languages. She began to recall all of the roadblocks, dead ends, the episodes at the State Department, airline flights, train rides. She had overcome so much just to get there. But now, nothing. No clues. No leads. No one to help.

"Was this all a cruel joke?" she wondered. "I just wanted to see Daniel. Just be with him for a while. Just explore what might have been. Is that asking so much? Are we really meant to be together? Will I ever find out?"

She started to feel dizzy, her jet lag, exacerbated by her relentless search for Daniel, catching up with her. Her pack seemed to have doubled in weight.

"I'd better go outside," she thought, stumbling toward the door, dragging her wheeled luggage and bumping several people who wondered who the beautiful woman was, moping around the climbing bureau. Bursting back into the daylight, she spotted a log bench a few meters away and slumped onto it.

Several minutes passed before she was able to compose herself. Even that was made difficult by the thin mountain air, at 1,600 meters. Everything seemed to be a barrier to her quest. It was too much. "I'll just find a hotel for tonight," she told herself, "and then go home..." Just as she felt tears might overcome her again she said to herself out loud, "Wait a minute, I'm on vacation too. Buck up, honey. Show 'em what you're made of!" Her inner resolve had come out on top and she became more determined to reach her goal.

As if on cue, a deep voice offered a welcome option, "Excuse me, Miss. May I be of assistance?"

Arianna spun around and, with a slight pause and furrowed brow, looked at the source of the intrusion. It was the man outside who exchanged glances with the cart driver. Just what she needed—a stalker! Maybe they were trying to corner her, or something. "How do I get out of this one?" Arianna groaned inwardly. "From the frying pan into the fire?"

The man looked very fit, like most everyone in the guide office. She estimated he was in his late 40s or early 50s. She also noticed his hiking outfit. "Hey," she said to herself. "Wasn't that the last guy to get off the train, just after the other guy who was walking in the opposidte direction of the Bahnhof?"

"Well," she began, not knowing how far to trust him, "I'm trying to find a friend of mine. He told me he would be climbing in the Zermatt area, and I was hoping this office might know where he is."

"My name is Jacques," the man continued. "My friends call me 'Jack'. It's my climbing name. Perhaps I can help you. What is your friend's name?"

"I…ahh…I'd rather not say," stammered Arianna, still recovering from her emotional moment. "Wait," she thought. "This might be apart of the security network the Secretary of State spoke of! Perhaps I should just play along for the moment."

"Do you know which mountain he was climbing?"asked Jacques.

"The Matterhorn. That's all I know."

"Umm…I see," Jacques murmured. "Often the arrangements made with the Führerverein are confidential, so it may be difficult to find out anything from them, even if they knew about your friend."

Jacques offered a spark of hope:

"I can show you some trails to hike, easy ones, that might connect you with parties ascending or descending the Matterhorn. At least you could pose some inquiries." He pulled a detailed trail map from his jacket pocket. "Would you be interested?"

"This guy speaks perfect English," she thought, "and at least he's trying to be helpful."

"Why, yes. That would be very useful," replied Arianna.

Taking a pencil from his shirt pocket, Jacques sat next to her.

Looking at her closely, he continued in a lower voice, "I would highly recommend this route here, through the section known as Hermettji-Alp." He highlighted one of the trails in pencil.

"It's part of the trail system that starts right at the south edge of town. The views are quite lovely, and you will eventually end up at the Schwarzsee, a small lake with a mountain hotel of the same name, a hike of four hours from here, with a gain of 950 meters. You will get great views of the Matterhorn, and once you arrive at the hotel, you can rest and take photos. There is a restaurant—bar, deck, a great place to view the mountain. Often, climbers stop there for a beer after returning from the mountain."

Arianna suppressed a gasp. Maybe she could learn about Daniel's climbing group from other climbers. "This man has indeed been helpful," she thought.

"You can take your time there and return by cable car back to Zermatt later in the afternoon," said Jacques.

"Why, thank you. I…ah…just might try your recommendation, *danke*," said Arianna, feeling elated by this new course of action and thankful Jack had contacted her.

"Do you have a hotel?" Jacques inquired.

"Not yet. Do you have any recommendations?"

"Why, yes, I do." Jacques pulled out his business card and wrote a name on the back. "The Hotel Alpenglo, on the Bahnhofstrasse. It is an excellent hotel. I know the proprietor there and the manager is named Laura. Tell them I sent you. They will give you an excellent price for a room. Their cuisine is outstanding as well. I wish you good fortune in your search, Miss. And I hope you have a pleasant stay in Zermatt."

They shook hands and Jacques returned to the Führerverein and Arianna turned to see the cart driver still waiting for her and called out to him, "Hotel Alpenglo."

He nodded and motioned her to climb aboard his electric cart. Two minutes later they arrived at the hotel and again Arianna tried to pay for her ride. "Oh, no, Miss. The hotel pays for the ride. It's the custom in Zermatt. Here, I can help with your bags."

"Oh, it's quite all right. I can manage. Thank you for waiting."

"My pleasure, Miss."

Arianna entered the Alpenglo and approached the front desk.

"Do you have a reservation?" the clerk inquired.

"No, but I was told to ask for Laura. Jacques, at the Führerverein recommended I stay here."

"Ahhh, yes. Just one moment, please. May I have your passport?" The clerk picked up his phone to make a request in German. Arianna caught the names 'Laura' and 'Jacques' in the brief exchange.

"Uh-oh," mused Arianna to herself as she glanced around the lobby. "This place looks a little on the expensive side. I may not be able to aff--"

An attractive brunette in her mid-thirties emerged from a back room and introduced herself with a smile. "Hello. My name is Laura. I'm the hotel manager. I heard Jacques sent you to our hotel."

"Why, yes. He was kind enough to give me a recommendation. I will probably just be needing a small room for one person."

"Well, well. Let's see what we have...Thomas, I'll handle this reservation, thank you. Ahh, this should do nicely. We have a queen bedroom on the fourth floor, with a view of the mountain. We are having a special promotion and the price is only 100 francs per night. Normally it would be 140 francs, so it's quite a nice deal. Now that includes a full continental breakfast every morning, full use of our gym, swimming pool, sauna, and half price on massage. Plus it includes your first night's dinner, free. Shall I arrange for your stay?"

Arianna thought, "Wow. I really would like to stay for at least three nights, especially in this place. And, hey, I'm on vacation." To Laura she said, "Yes, I'd like to stay for three nights," and handed over her credit card. Once Laura processed her check-in information, she handed the credit card back to Arianna along with two plastic key cards.

"Okay. Why don't I show you to your room. This way." She led Arianna to the fourth floor and opened the door to a room with a full view of the courtyard below and the Matterhorn in the distance. It was a stunning conclusion to an otherwise long day for the Seattle woman. "Dinner is open at 1830 hours. I look forward to seeing you," said Laura.

"Thank you. *Danke*. I'm sure I'll see you around," replied Arianna. As Laura departed, Arianna plopped down on the comforter-equipped bed and took in the view of the famous mountain. "Wow. Who would have convinced me this would be my destination when I was doing all that running around in Geneva?" she thought. "I think it's time for a nap, and then dinner. I'm starving."

Following a full course meal and a glass of wine in the Alpenglo dining room Arianna retired to her room and fell asleep in the luxurious bed, the window open to the mountain air.

After dark, a lone figure approached the view side of the hotel. He waited in the shadow of nearby trees for a half hour, making sure of the secrecy of his position.

He placed his hands on a drainpipe rising next to an open fourth floor window, his dark skin now clearly visible in the moonlight.

Noiselessly his soft-soled shoes supported his hand–over-hand action up the drainpipe and his confidence grew in reaching his sinister objective, just as Anatoly had instructed.

"All those hours tracking the woman who was the close friend of the man who defeated the *Irbis* team on the airliner," he breathed. His effort was about to pay off as he continued up the drainpipe, then...

"***Arrghh, ayeee***..." he screamed, and was hauled off the drainpipe from behind by strong hands with a vise-like grip. Then *"**Thud**,"* he was knocked unconscious from a blow to the back of his head!

Jacques quickly grabed the subdued figure under his armpits and hauled him into the shadow of nearby trees where he wraped duct tape around his mouth, feet and hands. He relieved the man of his Glock firearm with attached silencer, carried in a vest pocket.

No one in the hotel appeared disturbed by the brief nighttime scuffle.

Thankful that he had been vigilantly watching Arianna, Jacques stood over the man who had been tailing her on the train and all afternoon through Zermatt.

He removed his cell phone from his pocket and made a call...

CHAPTER 15

Ascent

Hörnlihütte   3,260 meters   10,695 feet
August 19, 2008
1900 hours

At dinner in the Hörnlihütte, Daniel, Tarkan, and Tom Renshaw met the guides who would accompany them up the mountain. Daniel was paired with a solid-looking man in his late thirties, with a positive, can-do expression and a pleasant demeanor.

"Klaus Altman," the guide said as he took Daniel's hand with a firm grip. "I look forward to taking you to the summit tomorrow. And, of course, bringing you back down as well," he added with a smile.

"Yes. Very nice to meet you, and thanks for reminding me about the most important part of the climb."

Altman's initial years as a Bergführer, or climbing guide, were centered around Grindelwald-Lauterbrunnental, where he led clients to the many summits in that area including the famous north face of the Eiger.

Built like a fireplug, he had numerous repeat clients who praised his easygoing, no-nonsense leadership style. His fellow Bergführern would recount his uncanny ability to know his clients' physical condition and change in attitude at all times during a climb. Altman had over twenty years of climbing guide experience and was fluent in four languages. Daniel instantly took a liking to him.

After a dinner heavy with carbohydrates, protein, and water, a brief discussion took place between the four Americans, two Turks, and four Bergführeren, noting key points of interest and danger on a map of the Matterhorn's Hörnligrat climbing route. Even though Thompson and Appleton, would not be climbing, it was important for them to know the intended route and to further acquaint themselves with the guides. Should anything go wrong, they would be the first to take action and coordinate any rescue activity from the Hütte.

The climbers would be grouped in pairs, each with a Swiss guide in the lead on the ascent and acting as an anchor on the descent. Daniel was paired with Altman, Tarkan with a guide named Wily, Mustafa would be roped up with Toni and Tom Renshaw would be in the trailing team with Max, who had climbed extensively with Klaus for several years.

Everyone headed to bed for an early sleep, knowing the guides would be awakening them at 0430 the next morning.

Daniel was still a little anxious and had difficulty falling asleep. "I don't know if I can do it," he fretted, while tossing in his bunk bed. "There's probably still ice on the ridge, the wind could easily pick up at this altitude, and I remember the cloud cover rolling in late in the afternoon. And how are we going to do those vertical sections?

"Even though I've dreamed of doing this since I was a boy I feel uneasy about the whole thing…"

Finally, the high altitude assisted him in arriving at a drowsy state, and he fell asleep.

All was dark and the Hütte had been still for several hours. Suddenly, a light appeared in one, then another, of its windows as activity commenced within. The hour was 0430 and the guides woke the climbers gently but firmly. As they attended to initial morning readiness, action began in the kitchen. Hot cereal, coffee, tea, and small fruit plates were prepared for guests.

For certain parties, special trail lunches were made, designed to be consumed in small portions at several points along the route. Bottles were filled with two liters of fresh water. The guides were first to finish breakfast and made sure their clients ate quickly. No time could be lost, considering the crunch of climbers attempting the summit that day.

When everyone finished, the guides performed a final inspection of their clients' packs. Headlamps were positioned and switched on, and each climber secured his boots and donned the appropriate outerwear.

"You put on fleece jacket now. No need for the windbreaker yet," said Klaus to Daniel. "And we will not need ice axes! Here, let me help you with this."

Quickly he wrapped two turns of a climbing rope around Daniel's waist, then secured the other end around himself, leaving three meters of slack between them. He glanced around to make sure Tarkan, Mustafa, and Tom were similarly roped up.

"No ice axes?" thought Daniel. "That must mean the route is clear of snow and ice! That is really good news."

"Okay, we go," announced Klaus, and all six men headed out. It was 0500 hours. With a gentle tug from Klaus, Daniel was propelled from the Hütte into the night.

Remembering the growing cloud cover from yesterday, Daniel expected his face to be pelted with rain or even snow driven by a stiff wind, common at this altitude. But after his first two steps he felt nothing. Only blackness punctuated by the beam of his headlamp.

Suddenly "Wh-a-at...?" Daniel was momentarily stunned. The light of a million stars filled the night, as if in a blazing send-off to their ascent! The sky was completely clear, the temperature an incredibly mild 45F, and there was *no wind!* None. It was a perfect climbing day!

Klaus and Daniel formed the lead rope team. Klaus had the most experience on this route, having made the Matterhorn ascent on the Hörnligrat ridge route over two dozen times. For the first fifty meters the route was level, and Daniel used the time to get used to following the beam of his headlamp.

Then, at 3,279 meters, the ascent began up a small, steep section, followed by a more moderate grade until the route settled in at a rough, class four scramble, able to be scaled with continuous use of both hands and both feet. The closeness of the rock made it easier for Daniel to see his way with the headlamp.

Klaus occasionally gave a gentle tug on the rope. Usually Daniel was able to immediately respond by picking up the pace. But sometimes he hesitated, searching past the dim glow of the headlamp for the route. It took a little while, but soon both guide and climber were fused into a synchronous routine and began to climb as one unit.

For the second time that day Daniel said to himself, "Good thing we have these guides. They're handy to have around if we get into a jam."

Upward, ever upward.

Occasionally, a pitch with high exposure presented itself. Klaus signaled Daniel to wait in a belaying position.

"That's good. Wait until I ascend a few meters," he shouted, while he climbed several meters farther.

The other three guides would use the same technique. At this point, Daniel knew he had enough rock climbing experience to instantly affix himself to a belay point in the rock, should Klaus falter or fall.

Then Klaus halted, and, positioning himself in a similar belay readiness, called for Daniel to continue. The two men repeated this process several dozen times during their ascent. Daniel began to see his guide's expertise lay not only in getting the climber from point A to point B, but in knowing when to exercise extreme caution, where the small refuges of safe belay were, and how to use them.

While some climbing leaders were expert at exercising "get-there-itis," Klaus and his Swiss guide mates were experts at "Get them up, but more importantly, make sure they get down."

Upward, hand over hand.

After thirty minutes, Daniel glanced to the east and saw a pale blue-green light on the horizon. "Helios is coming to bring us light and warmth," he surmised.

Slowly, slowly, the light in the east grew brighter, then began to change to a yellowish-orange, then deeper orange, and finally a deep red hue took over.

The rock in front of him and around him became a light gray and more visible. Daniel felt the rope gently go slack. Klaus shut off and removed his headlamp and urged Daniel to do the same. They resumed their upward trek, and, after fifteen more minutes, they were struck by the blazing glory of the fully-risen sun.

Upward, relentlessly upward.

A few minutes later they rounded a large boulder and Klaus halted again and announced, "We have reached the Solvayhütte! Four thousand meters altitude, just a little more than halfway up. We rest here for five minutes."

Daniel was able to see a small wooden hut, no bigger than an average living room. Heavily creosoted and weather-beaten, the Solvayhütte was built in 1916 as an emergency shelter for climbers stranded by weather or injury and had saved hundreds of lives since its construction.

Klaus showed Daniel the interior which was bare, except for an old wood stove with a small bundle of kindling beside it. There was no food or supplies.

Klaus related a story to Daniel, "I heard about some climbers a couple of years ago who were forced to spend three days here. The route was covered with ice. It was impossible for them to descend. Without the Solvayhütte, they would have died from the cold and altitude."

Both men took several gulps from their water bottles and ate a biscuit and dried fruit from their lunch sacks.

They exchanged a short greeting with Tarkan, Mustafa, Tom, and their guides, who were just arriving. Then Daniel and Klaus continued their upward ascent.

Zermatt   1,606 meters   5,269 feet
Hotel Alpenglo
August 20, 2008
0835 hours

"Yes, *danke*. I would like another cup of coffee. Thank you very much. "That was a very good breakfast," Arianna said to the attentive server. She marveled at the tastiness of her breakfast meal. So many fruits, and all kinds of cereal. "And how did they make that yogurt so creamy and tasty, ah…Fräulein…?"

"My name is Bridget," was the pleasant response, in perfect English. "Yes, it's very good isn't it? We make our own yogurt from local farms with pastures high in the Alps. The high altitude gives especially sweet milk and the farmers bring fresh supplies to us every day! Would you like a trail lunch to take with you today?"

"Why, yes. That would be most welcome. *Danke*, Bridget."

"Certainly. I'll return in a few minutes."

"Wow," thought Arianna. "I didn't know lunch was included. And a trail lunch at that. Her English is perfect, with an American touch to it. Maybe she attended a university in the U.S. After all, many European students did so."

In minutes, Bridget returned with an ample sack lunch and asked, "Are you headed toward the mountain today?"

"Yes. I'm trying to get to Schwarzsee today and return."

"I see you have a map. That hike is a favorite of mine. May I show you the trail I like the most?"

Bridget indicated her recommended route along the Mattervispa to Furi, then ascending moderately through the forests of Hermettji-Alp, eventually breaking out above tree line with continuous views of the Matterhorn, until arriving at Schwarzsee.

"*Danke.* I'll give that a try. Well, I should be off." Grabbing her pack, she stuffed the lunch inside. "*Auf wiedersehen. Danke.*"

"*Auf wiedersehen*, have a good hike," responded Bridget.

Arianna hefted her pack and headed out the door about 0930 hours, walking south on the Bahnhofstrasse. She was well prepared for a day in the mountains, with accessories provided by Laura: 30 SPF sunscreen, a wide-brim hiking hat from the hotel gift shop, and comfortable hiking boots rented from the equipment shop. She also carried the lunch from Bridget, a detailed map, and other gear from Seattle, including a rain jacket, a pile jacket, light gloves, sunglasses, a small first-aid kit, and a stainless-steel water bottle.

The temperature was a pleasant 64F with very light breezes and minimal clouds in the sky. A perfect day for hiking! At the south end of the paved walkway, she entered the trail system, surrounded by a dozen day hikers like herself. The trail followed the tail end of the Mattervispa and then turned off to the hamlets of Zum See and Furi, the latter being a major cable-car junction.

Soon the other hikers had peeled off to the dozens of trails in the area, and Arianna found herself alone in an extraordinarily beautiful Alpine setting with pines, firs and an occasional glimpse of the surrounding meadows of Rifflealp, Riffleberg, and the lower reaches of the Gornergrat, all to the east.

Every few minutes Arianna stopped to gaze at the scenery, and on one such occasion she glimpsed two hikers about fifty meters behind her that darted into the woods when she looked their way. "Am I being followed?" she wondered.

When it happened a second time, she became wary of an unwanted encounter.

Her mind raced, "Those people are following me. Who are they? Maybe they have guns! Sure wish I was with Daniel or even that Jacques fellow."

She quickened her pace as she ascended past the hamlet of Furi.

Sure enough. Whoever it was maintained a distance of fifty meters. "Who could it be?" she wondered. She didn't suspect anyone. Everybody had been so kind to her. "Why would …"

Then a realization hit her, the warning from the Secretary of State: there may still be a danger to your life and Daniel's from accomplices of the terrorists who hijacked the airliner.

Quickly she thought of a plan to foil her followers. Just ahead, about twenty meters, was a trail intersection. She quickly darted off the trail and concealed herself behind two pine trees and a fallen log.

"They won't know which branch of the trail I took. There's a chance I can give them the slip then get on another trail to Schwarzsee."

After a minute, two hikers passed close by her hiding place. They had dramatically quickened their pace when they discovered she was no longer in sight. When the pair reached the intersection, not knowing which direction she had taken, they made their best estimate of her route and followed the western trail branch, leading through the center of the Hermettji forest.

"That's odd," thought Arianna. "That's the direction both Jacques and Bridget suggested I go. I wonder if there's any connection…" But the thought seemed absurd. Both individuals had seemed so genuinely eager to help her, not harm her.

"So who the heck were these people?" She pondered for a moment. Then, consulting the trail sign, which expressed distances in hours, not kilometers, she chose another branch of the trail that angled upward and left, to avoid taking the trail taken by the two possible stalkers.

"I have plenty of time," she thought. "I can still reach Schwarzsee by mid-afternoon when climbers are supposed to arrive from descending the Matterhorn. I can ask around if they've seen Daniel."

Heading southwest up a slight incline in the trail, she continued to look behind her for several minutes for any sign of her pursuers.

The sun was high in the sky when Arianna decided to take a break for lunch beside a swiftly-flowing stream gurgling down a narrow gully. She started with the first of three thick slices of dark, hearty bread, spread with a creamy butter mixture provided in a small container. She added a slice of cheese to the second bread slice and took a swig from her water bottle.

"They sure know how to eat healthy, even on the trail," she thought, as she chose dried apricots and an apple for dessert. She would save the bar of Swiss chocolate at the bottom of her lunch sack for later.

The trail crossed the stream. she noted, "Hopefully it will start ascending a little more steeply on the other side." It was time to gain some elevation. As she hiked, she reminisced about her times with Daniel, when he taught her to read maps and be conscious of her position in the mountains.

She began crossing the rushing water by hopscotching on large rocks as the water swirled around her. At one point she hesitated, as no clear route appeared across the rocks, and she backtracked to try another approach. This time she was able to reach the other bank and ascended the southeast side of the gully.

She paused and turned to gain a view toward the southwest, and for the first time noticed several clouds forming in that direction over the summit of the Matterhorn.

It was early afternoon, about 1330 hours, and Arianna realized she might want to speed up her trek. Twenty minutes after the stream crossing, she noticed the trail becoming more and more indistinct until, finally, it seemed to peter out in a dead end! "What have I done? Where have I ended up?" she said to herself, with just the smallest bit of fear beginning to creep into her consciousness.

"This was a trail to Schwarzsee, wasn't it? No, wait, now that I recall, there wasn't any mention of Schwarzsee on the trail sign in this direction. I was so intent on avoiding those people, I didn't notice. Uh-oh. I must be on the wrong trail! That's why it didn't ascend more rapidly. I'd better go back!"

Hastily she retraced her route, and in another fifteen minutes reached the stream, a little out of breath.

At the stream she searched the rock formations for a way to cross, but the rocks looked different from this side. Well, she would just have to do her best, despite being in a hurry. She wouldn't mind if she got her feet a little wet. With a little more abandon in her stride, she approached the stream and skipped onto the first couple of rocks.

The water seemed to have gotten higher and louder. She wasn't sure it was the same stream she crossed a little while ago. Spying another nearby rock, she jumped to its flat surface.

But then she ran out of rocks. "Okay, I'll jump to that next one there," she muttered, eyeballing a rock about a meter away. She coiled and sprang desperately, putting speed before caution. Her right foot glided out and almost caught the flat surface of the rock, but her toe hit the side and she tumbled forward, both hands out to break her fall.

Splash! Into the icy water she went, plunging a half meter deep into the frigid glacier melt and getting completely wet, boots and all. Scrambling to the next set of rocks, the combination of wet and cold, and bewilderment at being on the wrong trail, caused fear to overcome her as she struggled out of the stream.

"I can't believe it. All this way to try and find Daniel and I end up getting soaked in a mountain stream, and I don't even know if he's up there or not! Am I just being stupid? He's probably not there anyway!"

After sitting on the ground on the northern bank of the stream in the shadow of the gully, she began to feel chilled. "I should have never come this far! I'll just go back to the hotel and make plans to go home. Daniel wasn't here anyway. And what am I doing in the middle of the freakin' Alps alone? That was stupid. What was I thinking?"

Then she remembered the fleece jacket and fished for it in her pack and put in on. She wolfed down a quarter of the chocolate bar in one bite. After a minute she thought, "That was good. I'll have another bite." In a few minutes she began to feel her energy return. She strapped her pack on and headed back down the trail, noting the buildup of clouds had progressed further since she first noticed it a half hour earlier.

Solvayhütte   4,000 meters   13,123 feet
August 20, 2008
0638 hours

For the next hour Klaus and Daniel ascended with only one short break. They successfully scaled a vertical wall, the upper Moseley slab, about four or five meters high, assisted by a thick fixed rope placed to aid climbers and prevent dangerous bottlenecks of climbing teams on both the ascent and descent.

After reaching the top of the wall, Daniel noted with great relief the absence of any ice or snow on their route. All this time their position on the Hörnli ridge had obscured their view of the summit. But just then, after rounding a large outcropping,

Bam!

The summit came into full view, only about a hundred meters away!

The other six in their party were not far behind. "We're gonna make it!" Daniel exulted to himself.

A stiff breeze from the southwest kicked up and Klaus halted for a moment. "Put on your windbreaker," he commanded.

The scrambling grew easier as the ridgeline eased another ten degrees from its previous steepness. Klaus and Daniel were now in a walking mode, getting ever closer to the summit where someone had fashioned a makeshift banner of small multi-colored nylon flags, now dancing wildly in the wind. Fifty meters, forty meters, thirty…

Then Klaus called a halt and pointed directly ahead of them. "We must be careful," he cautioned. "Ice. Put on crampons," and they stopped to affix the spikey contraptions to their boots.

One slip and it would be a 2,500-meter fall to the rock on the sheer east face below. But their practice of belaying each other paid off again. Klaus proceeded three meters, then positioned himself next to solid rock with multiple places to serve as friction points for the rope. He and Daniel traded positions three times as they continued the final portion of the ascent. Finally Klaus stopped within five meters of the summit and said, "Daniel, we wait for Tarkan, then you go all the way to the top. We can take off our crampons for the summit."

Tarkan and his guide arrived five minutes later. He and Daniel took the lead in front of their guides and made a dozen steps through the snow which now covered the ice.

Both simultaneously climbed to the rock outcropping of the highest point, locked in solidarity. One arm around the other, they both raised their other arms in triumph.

The summit of the Matterhorn, 4,478 meters above the sea!

Five minutes later, Mustafa and his guide arrived, then Tom and his guide. All stood on the summit, still roped to their individual guides. The four high-fived each other, then did an embrace while Klaus took pictures with a small digital camera. Following this display of male camaraderie, each of the climbers posed on the summit with his individual guide while others snapped their picture.

They all backed off the summit and allowed room for other climbers to stand atop the highest point. The guides encouraged them to munch a small bit of bread or fruit and drink two cups of water.

Matterhorn Summit   4,478 meters,   14,691 feet
August 20, 2008
0900 hours

Descent

With the moment of triumph over, the guides prepared their clients for the trip down. "Okay, everybody take out your crampons and re-attach them to your boots," said Klaus. "We will only need them for a little while, but they must be tight. Going down this part has the greatest danger!" Clients and guides alike spent five minutes wrestling with their crampons while the guides double-checked the climbers' boots. "Okay, we go down now," said Klaus, motioning Daniel forward into the lead position.

When descending, the most experienced climber on the rope always had the uphill position, allowing him to make an arrest of his partner should a fall occur. The guides, being intimately familiar with the best belay points, were always the last to descend on each rope team. And so it went, the first climber descending.

The four rope teams were separated by five meters, a measure of safety in dealing with potential rock fall.

After repeating their crampon exercise for twenty meters of ice the climbers stowed their pronged footgear and began the treacherous downward trek on rock.

Klaus and Daniel were the first team to move downward. As he turned to watch Klaus descend Daniel noted that Mustafa was quick to immediately follow Klaus, even though it was Tarkan's turn to take second rope position.

"That's odd," thought Daniel. "I wonder why he did that? Is Mustafa in a hurry to get down?"

Daniel put this observation together with other things he had noticed about Mustafa accompanied by the nagging feeling that something wasn't quite right.

He mused, "Mustafa had only recently met Tarkan who enjoys climbing with him. But maybe there's more to this man than Tarkan has yet to discover. His continual traveling between Russia and Turkey is another oddity. And what part of Russia is he from…?"

The descent now steepened enough to force the climbers to employ 'downclimbing' techniques, turning their bodies into the rock and using both hands and feet to edge down the ridge.

Daniel quickly stopped worrying about Mustafa as the most treacherous section of the ridge abruptly presented itself, the vertical face of the Moseley Slab.

But Mustafa had not forgotten about Daniel! He had been presented with $150,000 by Anatoly at their Istanbul coffee meeting as a downpayment with another $150,000 to follow if he dispatched Daniel and made it look like a climbing accident. "Now is the time," Mustafa breathed as he was the closest to Daniel and the other rope teams were not yet visible.

Daniel, still in the lead, halted at the top of the slab with Klaus standing next to him.

Daniel fished in his right pocket for the leather gloves to help him down the thick fixed rope, dangling on the face of the slab.

Both Daniel and Klaus took a brief moment to gaze at the glaciers below them, a mere 2,000 meter freefall away when they were joined by Mustafa and the Swiss guide, Toni, who had just completed the prior section of the downclimb, well ahead of the other climbers.

"Strange," said Daniel to Klaus. "I hadn't realized they were that close to us," rekindling his anxiety about Mustafa's behavior.

Daniel bent down to grasp the upper section of the fixed rope to descend face-in to the rock, with Klaus positioning himself to belay him with the climbing rope.

Suddenly they heard a scuffle and a muffled cry from Toni.

Klaus whirled around only to see Toni slumped over, holding his gut, with their severed rope dragging behind Mustafa who had leaped to the top of the slab with a bloodied knife in his right hand. Before Klaus could react, Mustafa, coming in low, shoved Klaus off the rock and out into thin air.

"*Heyyyy, Falling*!" yelled Klaus as he fell off the rock, helpless to stop himself from plummeting to his death. Still tied to Daniel, he released the slack in the rope, letting it fall free.

To his horror Daniel instantly realized his own danger. He was roped to Klaus and would have no chance of stopping the momentum of Klaus' weight falling down the slab face.

He only had time for one move before he would be pulled into the void.

Seeing a small rock outcropping just to his left, in a flash he whipped two loops of the slack climbing rope with his left hand over the horn-like rock and held on tight.

"*Thwaap*," the climbing rope jerked taut but held the two men from falling farther, but Daniel was pulled off the fixed rope and toward the rock horn.

In a moment, Daniel recovered, but the impact had also jolted his memory...

The Snow Leopard had returned!!!,

"This must be an attempt by the *Irbis* team to strike in revenge for foiling their attack on the airliner."

For a few seconds the two men dangled from the climbing rope on the slab face beyond Mustafa's view.

Both Klaus and Daniel were in a swinging motion between the rock horn and the fixed rope, and on the return swing Daniel was able to grab the thick rope and hang on with both hands.

Daniel listened intently for any indicator of Mustafa's presence above him, knowing he would try to cut or dislodge the thinner climbing rope from the rock horn, sending he and Klaus into oblivion. Sure enough, he detected the sounds of boots scuffling to his left. It was now or never!!!

Still facing inward toward the slab face and clenching the fixed rope with both hands, Daniel jammed the toes of both boots into small crevices near the top of the slab. In a lightning fast move he rose up on his toes and hauled himself up on the fixed rope with his hands.

Mustafa was surprised by the sudden presence of his adversary rising on his left while his main attention was on the climbing rope around the rock horn, to the right.

At the top of his leap Daniel reached for Mustafa's open throat with his right hand, not to strangle him as Mustafa initially thought, but to grab the front of his shirt and jacket. Daniel's left hand swung swiftly at Mustafa's right arm keeping the knife at bay.

With all his strength he dragged the assassin over the edge of the slab and away from the rock, both men now in mid air!

After a second had passed, Daniel released his hold on Mustafa as he passed overhead. The terrorist's flailing body now accelerated toward the glacier below.

But Daniel was still attached to the climbing rope!

*"**Aiyyyy!**"* yelled Mustafa, the sound echoing nearly the whole distance down the mountain's steep east face.

*"**Uhhhh,**"* grunted Daniel as the climbing rope tugged at his mid section, slamming him into the slab face.

"Hey, anyone down there?" someone yelled from above. It was Tom Renshaw who had finally arrived at the top of the slab along with his guide, Max, and the rope team of Tarkan and Wily.

"We're down here," yelled Daniel. "Help us back up."

The surprised climbers looked over the slab edge to see Daniel and Klaus dangling in mid-air on their climbing rope, still looped around the life-saving rock horn.

In short order the other climbers hauled the stricken men to the top of the slab.

Turning their attention to Toni, the wounded guide, they realized the knife thrust had missed the center of his abdomen and his injury was treatable with bandages and antibiotic cream. Toni could still walk with difficulty and he joined Max's rope, letting Tom Renshaw complete the rest of the descent unroped, an arrangement Klaus approved of, noting Tom's extensive and recent climbing experiences.

"I thought it was all over when Mustafa shoved Klaus off the slab," said Daniel, still breathing heavily, as the other men listened to his synopsis of events in amazement.

Still stunned from the experience, Klaus took a few seconds to compose himself. "Thank God Daniel had the presence of mind to get the rope around that rock horn. Glad I let go of the loose coils I had been holding."

The two men held each other closely for several seconds before the others helped them back away from the slab edge.

Tarkan shook his head, at first disbelieving his new friend would try such an attack. But Daniel said, "There were a number of things that didn't seem right about him," and revealed the other observations he'd made about Mustafa's behavior and surmised this was a 'fifth column' attempt by the *Irbis* organization to exact revenge for the failed airliner hijacking.

Tarkan finally nodded assent and professed he didn't know all that much about Mustafa's background.

After several minutes of recovery the climbers carefully descended the fixed rope to the safety of the climbing route below the slab face. Daniel and Klaus rested at the base of the Moseley Slab, to let their adrenaline subside.

"After all," said Daniel, "Surviving a murder attempt on the Matterhorn wasn't a typical climbing experience."

Gingerly they made their way down to the Solvayhutte where they took a break and re-examined Toni's wounds.

Eight hundred meters below the Solvayhütte, the Hörnlihütte came into view and Daniel realized the end was near. All the climbers reached the safety of the Hornlihutte in another hour.

Coincident with feelings of relief at the completion of his lifelong quest to climb the Matterhorn, Daniel wondered about Arianna and what she might have experienced following his dramatic rescue of the hijacked passengers. He felt more confident about finally telling her his feelings.

He was still thinking of Arianna when he noticed the clouds beginning to slowly form over the top of the Matterhorn.

"Must have moved up from the Italian side," he thought, recalling their earlier formation in the southern valley below the mountain.

Klaus excused himself and entered the Hutte to report the death of Mustafa to the Uberbergfurher along with the circumstances. After hearing the story the head guide repeated most of the report on the radio to the Fuhrerverein in central Zermatt and came out to advise Daniel and Klaus to make a full report to the police after reporting in at the Fürherverein.

Thompson and Appleton, the security agents who remained at the Hornihutte were quick to pass liters of fresh water and buttered sweet biscuits to the climbers, to replace some of the carbohydrates burned off during the momentous climb.

"We'll have plenty of time to drink beers this evening at the bar," announced Tom. "Let's rest here, have lunch, and head down to the Schwarzsee at about 1300 hours. You boys have earned a free trip on the cable car from Schwarzsee down to Zermatt. Its on me!"

"Can they make cable car come to Hörnlihütte?" Tarkan asked. Laughter and jokes from the rest of the team met his remark. Daniel was just happy to be down and safely out of the area of dangerous exposure. He downed a full liter of water and two buttered biscuits and was still ready for a sandwich lunch.

Afterward, Daniel leaned back against the walls of the Hörnlihütte and took a short nap, his body temporarily spent from the ferocious ascent and descent and the attempt on his life. There had been 8,000 feet of vertical gain and loss compressed into six hours.

It seemed like only seconds went by before he heard Tom's voice, "All right, Gentlemen. Start your engines. It's 1300 hours. Let's head on down to Schwarzsee." Just before departing they shook hand with their guides and gave their farewells, deeply thankful for their expertise and care.

CHAPTER 16
Rendezvous

~·~◦❀❀❀◦~·~

Furi   1,972 meters   6,470 feet
August 20, 2008
1545 hours

In retracing her route one kilometer, Arianna slowly realized her mistake. She took time to double-check her position on the map, silently berating herself for not doing so earlier.

"Daniel taught me always to be aware of my position both on the trail and on the map. Boy, did I blow that one. Those people pursuing me must have really had me rattled. I should have gone uphill and west, at that last trail sign, not south. If I go west now I'll ascend moderately through the Hermettji forest and get on the ridge trail to Schwarzsee."

She checked the map again. "Oh, that stream was the Furggbach, coming from the FurggGletscher. No wonder that water was cold! I should arrive at Schwarzsee in time to see most of the climbing parties...

"Oh, no! It's 1550 hours! Many of the climbers may be starting their descent by now. I might miss Daniel's!"

She quickened her pace from Furi to the woods in the Hermettji-Alp and put the pursuing incident out of her mind as a secondary issue in comparison with finding Daniel.

Just before reaching the switchback section of the Hermettji-Alp she cast another glance at the sky while in the middle of a clearing. The clouds had turned darker now, and there were no blue patches visible. A new concern entered Arianna's head: if inclement weather hit, the climbers were likely to take the cable car down and she would miss Daniel's party if they did so. She continued to ascend energetically with no stops to rest, despite it being her first day at altitude, an important factor adding to her growing fatigue. But she was warming up now, and stuffed her fleece jacket in her pack.

Hotel Schwarzsee 2,583 meters 8,474 feet
August 20, 2008
1550 hours

The climbing team negotiated a small switchback, winding south along the Hörnligrat ridge to a scree slope just under a cliffy section of the ridge. All party members could now clearly see the Schwarzsee Hotel about 200 meters below, and in twenty minutes they were standing on the hotel's deck where three dozen climbers and day hikers were gathered, taking in a late afternoon beer.

Daniel's team grabbed the nearest two tables and dumped their packs. "Thees more like it," Tarkan trumpeted. "Now we talking! Fräulein, I need two brewskies," he told the comely barmaid who came out to serve them, not knowing that his Americanized choice of words for 'beer' would be completely lost on European ears.

Between guffaws, Steve Thompson explained the confusion to the young, pretty Swiss server, who laughed and took drink requests from the remaining team members. "*Danke schön,* Vicki," said Steve, before she disappeared inside the hotel to fill their order.

Daniel sat on the end of the deck bench, next to Tarkan. Their beers arrived and the climb team hoisted their mugs in triumph and toasted each other. The drink gave Daniel a temporary reprieve from his fatigue and he took his first glance at the surroundings on the deck. The patrons all seemed like outdoor types, most likely day-hiking in the area.

"Gentlemen," a voiced boomed from behind them. "I'm Gerry Trapper, freelance journalist. You must be the Renshaw party." The man was dressed in day hiking clothes and carried a day pack along with two expensive-looking cameras, one slung over each shoulder.

Immediately Tom Renshaw jumped into a position between the climbing party and the intruder, appearing cautious but relaxed as the man looked to pose no harm and even had his hand extended to make a handshake. Tom shook his hand firmly and said, "Nice to meet you. I don't mind you taking photos but I ask that you stay 3 meters away from my climbing party. They've just descended from the Matterhorn."

"Sure," said Trapper. "No problem. Any chance I might get to talk with anyone who was on the climb? Say, weren't there supposed to be six of you?"

"I'm afraid you'll have to wait until this evening when we're at our hotel in Zermatt, say after 2000 hours? The guys are still a bit bushed from the climb. I'm sure you can appreciate that. You can take all the photos you want here."

"Thanks. I'll do that and look forward to taking you up on that invitation this evening."

Tom did not look ruffled at this interruption. He had anticipated there would be publicity seekers immediately after the descent and felt the security risk was low for both Daniel and Tarkan in this case.

Daniel noted the professional way Tom had handled the intruder and was about to return to the conversation at the table when he spied a face he thought he recognized. By chance, the man's gaze met his in the same instant but he quickly turned away and ducked behind another group of hikers, as if he didn't want to be recognized. Daniel's curiosity heightened.

He mused, "Where had he seen that face? Was it in the hotel? On the train? At the Hornlihutte? The man's mustache looked very familiar." His first reaction was to report the incident to Tom Renshaw. But as he turned to speak to Tom his brain made the connection!

Security team! That was it! He had seen the man on the security team during his visit to the White House and State Department in Washington, D.C.

"But, why would the State Department send another agent or team to Zermatt without being part of Tom's detail?" he thought. "Logic would dictate they should all be working together. Was there something Tom wasn't telling him? Something that was being hidden from him?" Daniel decided to find out on his own and, grabbing his pack, excused himself from the table to visit the toilet.

He approached the man from the side so as to surprise him. "Hi, I'm Daniel Prescott. I remember you were part of the White House Secret Service and the security team at the State Department a week ago."

Caught off guard, the man stammered, "Oh…Oh yes… Ahh.."

Daniel decided he would learn more by putting the man at ease. "I really appreciated your help when I visited the President and Secretary of State. She was quite helpful in getting me to understand U.S. objectives with international partners."

"Yes, she's really good at that," he replied. Then, realizing it was foolish to continue any pretenses, he volunteered, "I'm Jim Fowler. *Agent* Jim Fowler. I'm here on a special assignment for the Secretary."

"Well, why don't you sit with the rest of the team? They're right over there," said Daniel, gesturing to the west end of the deck with the best view of the Matterhorn. It was then he noticed more dark clouds moving in from the south, over the top of the mountain.

Fowler hesitated. "Ahh… I…ahh…I'm actually supposed to remain separate from the main climbing team. Actually, I might as well tell you now since you can verify all of this with Agent Renshaw. I was sent here with several other agents to watch over Miss Reynolds. The Secretary thought she might discover your destination and try to find you. This is completely outside our normal protocol providing security just for you, given your new national status."

Daniel could not comprehend what he just heard. "*Miss Reynolds*? Arianna Reynolds? Wha...she...she's here...in Zermatt? Right now...?"

"Yes. In fact she was ascending the trail from Hermettji to this location, the Schwarzsee, when we lost sight of her a couple of hours ago. Another agent and I were behind her but kept a discrete distance so as not to be discovered.

"The Secretary didn't want her to know about our detail, as she's not yet a fully authorized contact for you. We only had time in Washington, D.C. to do a cursory check to make sure it was okay for her to meet the Secretary. Several other procedures remained before we could allow her to contact you. You must realize you have the highest security threshold in our system. The same as the President!"

Still baffled, Daniel asked, "You said there were other agents watching her as well?"

"Yes. A retired climbing guide named Jacques, who watched her on the train, all the way from Geneve, and at the Fürherverein, in Zermatt. Then there was a baggage cart driver, Henri. At the Hotel Alpenglo she came under the auspices of Laura, the manager, another of our contract agents brought in from Zurich, as well as Bridget, also from Zurich.

"They had all been doing an excellent job as contact agents until Ingrid and I lost sight of her on the trail awhile ago. We scoured all possible venues then came up here, hoping to spot her."

Daniel was still stunned at the news.

"I believe she's trying to find you, hoping you would be descending from the mountain. The Secretary ordered us, today, to form a level three protection detail for her, a similar protection we had authorized for you. Unfortunately, she slipped through our fingers."

"Yes. Yes. I understand now," said Daniel. He could swear the temperature had dropped a good ten degrees in the last few minutes.

"And she was out there somewhere," he thought. "Lost, but probably not too far away."

His mind accelerated, "Because of the coming storm I should find her, immediately. If the security people catch up to me, fine. But there isn't time to inform everyone and do proper 'protocol.'"

"Ahh, …Jim, I have to find the toilet," he said. Why don't you advise Agent Renshaw what you told me? I'll join all of you in a few minutes."

"Will do," said Fowler, and he turned to join Tom Renshaw and the climbing team, just as his partner, Ingrid emerged from the hotel. He motioned for her to join him.

Daniel hefted his pack and disappeared inside the hotel, quickly discovering an exit out the back. His prior scan of the map showed the main trail to the forested region below was on the ridge just to the south of Schwarzsee. He headed for it at a fast walk, careful to keep out of sight of the deck.

Despite his fatigue from the punishing climb earlier in the day, Daniel bounded down the ridge, aware Arianna was likely fatigued and limited in her ability to exert at altitude. About halfway down the ridge he felt the first drops of cold rain on his bare hands and the force of a rising wind at his back.

Meanwhile, Tom Renshaw listened intently to the update on Arianna and asked, "Jim, did you tell Daniel that Arianna was here and you lost sight of her on the trail below?"

"Of course, Tom. I figured he would ask you anyway, so I couldn't lie about our mission or her status. He would have eventually found out the truth."

"Did you know what he might do if he found out she's missing or in trouble? Did you tell him on which trail you last saw her?"

"Ahh… Yes.. I told him we lost her on the Furi – Hermettji trail."

"He might go to any lengths to find her, even as fatigued as he is from the climb. Where is he now?"

"Well, about five minutes ago he was going to the toilet and …."

Tom scanned the crowd on the deck and said, "He's not here, and I'll bet he's not going to the toilet either. We have two missing people now. Best we get everyone mobilized to search for both of them."

Aware that the weather was rapidly changing, Tom cut short the round of beers and organized his team into three groups, issuing orders politely but firmly.

"Folks, Jim Fowler, one of our security agents, was assigned to track Arianna Reynolds, a close friend of Daniel's, on the trail system below this hotel. Daniel just heard about this and has departed to look for her. They are both likely in sub-optimal condition and we need to find them and get them to safety, given this approaching storm.

"Tarkan, you have already completed a challenging day, I want you to take the next cable car back to Furi and wait for the rest of us there.

"Jim and Ingrid, you are to descend the small northern loop of the Hermettji-Schwarzsee trail, in case Arianna might have taken that route. Wait for the rest of us at Furi."

Tom pulled out his map and pointed out trails and directions. "Steve, you and Joseph will descend the southern loop of the Hermettji-Schwarzsee trail, via Furgg and continue down to Furi.

"I will take the Hermettji trail along the ridge, in hopes of finding both Daniel and Arianna holed up in the trees for protection from the coming storm.

"We'll all meet at the Furi cable car station no later than 1800 hours. Okay, its 1600 hours now. Everyone has their rain gear, right? Then, we're off!"

Everyone donned their packs and headed out to their respective assignments. Tom watched the team disperse and reminded himself that they were supposed to ensure Arianna's security as well as Daniel's. Fortunately, everyone was an expert mountaineer and knew how to take care of themselves, even in marginal conditions.

The time was 1610 hours. Studying the gathering dark clouds, Daniel wondered if he made the right choice to descend alone. No matter now. As he reflected on his summit success, he found himself thinking, "Is this all there is? Are there no more goals after this? After all, I've been through a huge number of challenges, several of them life threatening.

"Maybe I'll do a few speeches for the President's and Secretary's programs? What else is there?"

The trail through a scree field was completely open to the elements, and Daniel knew it was dangerous to get caught in an exposed position, mainly because of the threat of lightning during thunderstorms, which were common this time of year. As he rounded a small switchback a light rain began to fall. The tree line was about a hundred meters away.

As he descended the remainder of the scree slope Daniel shot a glance to the west and was shocked at how the weather had changed. The Matterhorn now appeared like a giant white fang, reared against a charcoal-black sky.

Returning to an analytical mode he thought, "There's something not quite right. Tom must train his people pretty well. They shouldn't have lost sight of her. Maybe she sensed they were following her and concluded they might have been up to no good. She could've taken evasive action, maybe gone off trail.

"Maybe, but it wouldn't be like her to do that", he reasoned. "In all the hikes we had taken together she was always practical and never pushed a risky option. If she did go off- trail, it may have been only temporarily, and she likely got back on it, attempting to go higher, trying for Schwarzsee."

But a bigger question remained in his mind. "Why is she here? What possessed her to journey to this place? I thought our presence was supposed to be secret? Why did she …?"

He paused and his heart leapt at the conclusion, "Maybe she really missed me while I was gone. Maybe …"

The rain began to intensify and forced him to stop for a minute to don his rain jacket. He made another quick check of the map and continued his rapid pace down the ridge toward the forest of the Hermettji-Alp. The light faded with the onset of heavier rain and darkening clouds. No longer confident his wide-brim hiking hat would shed the increasing deluge, Daniel stuffed it into his pack and pulled a pile cap over his head, along with the hood of his rain-jacket, as he entered the upper woods on the first leg of six switchbacks, angling to the right.

Hermettji-Alp   2,053 Meters   6,676 Feet
August 20, 2008
1634 hours

The rain began to fall on Arianna as she ascended the trail in the Hermettji forest.

Annoyed at the rain she yelled to herself in frustration, "Is there anything else that can get in my way? Had all these obstacles happened because I was not meant to find him? Then we're not meant to be together, was that it? Well, why don't I just give up now? What's the point? Isn't it time to go back to Zermatt and head home?"

She continued to entertain doubts as she realized it would be foolish to continue hiking in open terrain, considering the danger of thunderstorms and lightning. Sure enough, off in the distance she heard a low rumble. Thunder! At least she was in the shelter of this forest for the moment.

But the map showed the trail ascending through open country on a ridge. Very dangerous, and she was quite fatigued. She recalled some of Daniel's guiding words from their numerous day hikes together: 'Be aware of fatigue when combined with severe weather changes like rain or snow. It accelerates the effect of chills.' She said aloud to herself, "Speaking of chills, it seems ten degrees colder than just a little while ago."

She approached the first of several switchbacks and saw two signs at an intersection. The upper board read 'Furgg 1.5 Std, Schwarzsee 1.75 Std' and pointed along a trail heading south along an easy upward grade. She contemplated the second sign, which read, 'Schwarzsee 1.0 Std.' It pointed toward a dog-leg right or north, with a slightly steeper grade. "Daniel would likely be taking the shortest route down," she theorized, so she would go on the right leg. She recognized the roar of a nearby waterfall and thought, "I wonder if that's the same stream I fell into down below? Guess I better put on my rain jacket."

The rain and wind grew steadily harder as Arianna struggled to pull her rain jacket out of her pack on the side of the trail. As she gave a final tug on the jacket, a gust of wind grabbed it from her hands and sent it tumbling into the brush off the trail. Her first instinct was to jump after it before it could get blown farther away.

But the diminished light and rain prevented her from seeing beyond the first branches of brush. As she planted her feet in the vegetation to grab at her parka, she felt the strange sensation of having nothing solid under her feet. Too late! There was a small cliff just behind the brush, with a gulley that connected to the rocky stream where a waterfall plunged down a rock chasm nearly twenty meters deep!

With a cry of surprise and fear, Arianna tumbled down a steep scree and brushy slope onto a narrow ledge, landing with a **Thump** just beside the turbulent waterfall. A fall from the ledge would end on the rocks at the base of the falls, a good ten meters below. She suffered a few scrapes but was otherwise unhurt.

The pouring rain continued to add to her predicament before it turned to a mix of rain and snow. Still without her rain parka, she began to shiver as she searched the rocks above the ledge for a route back to the trail. None appeared accessible.

The rain intensified, forcing Daniel to pull the bib of his rain jacket lower over his head, limiting his vision to one meter in front of his feet. Big snowflakes mixed with the rain made it difficult to distinguish the end of the right-angled switchback, but he was able to make the 170-degree turn onto the next leg of the trail. The rain and snow pelted even harder, as if to prevent him from making his descent. The wind had picked up dramatically and began to blow everything horizontally, forcing Daniel to draw his jacket hood even tighter, further restricting his vision.

The storm's darkness deepened, and another rumble of thunder scattered what was left of Arianna's fragile composure. The heavy snow accumulated on her hair and light hiking shirt and began to cling to the fabric of her pack, still a good four meters above her on the side of the trail.

Her pack was the only indicator of her presence on the ledge below. She yelled for help but her voice was drowned out by the deafening roar of the waterfall. Even with her chilled bare hands tucked under her armpits she began to shiver.

At the same moment Daniel completed the fourth leg of the six-switchbacks. As he started down the fifth, he heard the noise of the waterfall above the howling of the wind and pounding of the rain. The storm's intensity still forced him to keep his parka visor low, and he halted to put on his gloves.

Just below him, Arianna gave up her struggle to regain the trail. There were no handholds, no avenues of escape. No one could hear her over the rushing water, made even louder by the runoff from the storm. She shivered uncontrollably and cowered against the wall of the ledge. It was only a matter of time before hypothermia gained the upper hand and shut down her body functions.

Daniel resumed his pace on the fifth switchback and made the turn to descend the sixth when he noted a significant snow accumulation had already taken place on this section of the trail. One rock in particular already had several centimeters of…

He stopped dead in his tracks! What was that shiny metallic substance on the rock, not yet covered by the snow? A pop can thrown away by a careless hiker? Seemed like an odd position for a pop can. He took a step to his right for a closer look. That was no rock!

Brushing the snow away from the colored metal object, he discovered it was a backpack with a metallic piece on its flap.

It was an image of an animal: a bull, Taurus! ***The pin he gave Arianna in Seattle!*** Furiously he brushed the rest of the snow away to discover her backpack was partially opened.

He yelled her name, hoping she was nearby, but there was no answer. Only the roar of the nearby waterfall. He yelled again. No response.

He began a search of the immediate area, carefully avoiding the cliff hidden by brush just off the trail. He thought, "I wonder if …", and, as he parted the bushes he gazed down into the gully leading to the stream, he saw her, backed against the rock wall on the ledge, a good four meters below him.

He yelled again, this time bellowing her name over the din of the waterfall. Startled, she looked up to see just his head peeking over the edge of the gully. She had never seen such a welcome sight and responded in a feeble voice, "Daniel! Can you get me out of here? I'm freezing!"

"Okay," he replied at the top of his lungs. "Give me a few minutes." His mind madly contemplated the best options for her rescue. He retreated to the trail and removed his pack, setting it next to hers, the rain and snow showing no sign of abating. He debated with himself as he rummaged through his pack.

"I could use my rain pants, my fleece jacket…no, that won't quite be enough…ah …but I could add her fleece jacket, it's still in her pack. Strange, I don't see her rain jacket and she's not wearing it. Might have blown away….wait, there it is, stuck in those bushes!" He gathered her jacket and tied all the clothing together, making a large knot at the bottom.

Returning to the gully's edge, he threw the line of clothes down to her, but the wind made it difficult for her to grasp it. Finally she caught a hold of the knot and pulled the line toward her.

"Can you hang on? I'll pull you up," he yelled, recognizing her chilled hands might not be up to the task.

"I think so," she cried.

"Here goes," replied Daniel. He began to pull on the line of clothes, making sure his feet were dug into the turf at the edge of the cliff. Slowly she lifted off the ledge as he strained to pull her weight. She was a half meter above the ledge when suddenly Daniel felt the earth under his feet give way in a cascade of dirt and small stones.

"Falling!" he yelled, the automatic response of a climber who loses his footing. Still looking upward when Daniel began to fall, Arianna crashed back to the ledge causing the line to go slack. "*Uhhhhh,*" she groaned as she made a hard landing.

In that same instant, Daniel began to fall…

Thwapp!

Another hand appeared from the darkness and grabbed Daniel by the wrist, suspending him in midair.

Tom Renshaw!

Tom had seen the two packs by the side of the trail and discovered Daniel struggling with an unseen load. The noise of the falls had masked the sound of Tom's approach, and as he neared Daniel to assist, the ground caved in and Tom simultaneously grabbed a nearby tree and reached for Daniel's wrist as he fell.

"Tom! Thank God you found me!"

Hauling Daniel back up, Tom waited for Daniel to grab another small tree before releasing the hold on his wrist. Daniel's right hand still held the slack clothes rope, which he quickly tucked under his belt, freeing both hands.

But then, ***Craaack!*** The tree Tom clung to broke off, sending him toward the abyss!

Fortunately, Daniel was positioned close enough to Tom to grasp the shoulder strap of his pack with his right hand and haul him back to the safety of the gully's edge.

Together, Tom and Daniel pulled Arianna off the ledge again, this time succeeding in hoisting her all the way to the tree and safety.

"Daniel," she cried. "Daniel, my God, Oh my God." The two hugged each other tightly, like they would never let go. Tom Renshaw backed away discreetly to give them privacy.

Daniel realized she was still shivering and untied her fleece jacket and rain parka from the clothes line to wrap around her. As he did so they gazed into each other's eyes with *the* look.

"Oh, Daniel," she whispered, "I thought I had lost you. Forgive me for not seeing you for the complete man you are. I think my world would have come to an end without you. I just *had* to find you!"

Daniel simply said, "For a long time *you* have been my world."

Then he pulled her into his arms again and they kissed for the first time since their friendship began, three years earlier. Their hands held each other's faces, still gazing with stars in their eyes.

Realizing Tom had given them crucial assistance, Daniel broke away momentarily and approached the security agent with arms extended to engage in a *mano-a-mano* hug, the kind reserved for extreme gratitude and a job well done.

"Arianna, this is Tom Renshaw, U.S. State Department security," said Daniel. "He and his people have been watching you for the past two days, just to make sure you were safe. It was his agents who followed you on the trail and who were part of the hotel staff."

With great relief Arianna added, "Well you sure did your job today! Thank you, Tom. You were just in the nick of time." She followed her words with a grateful hug.

Just then, the sky began to lighten and the wind, rain and snow subsided.

"I'll go on ahead and meet you at the Furi cable car station," said Tom, as he grabbed his pack and got a head start down the trail.

Daniel and Arianna re-stuffed their packs and turned to follow him, walking side by side down the trail, their arms still locked around each other. Their fatigue temporarily forgotten, the weight of their packs non-existent, the mud puddles now a playful hopscotch rather than a hindrance.

Unable to take their eyes and hands off each other, every twenty steps brought another embrace and kiss.

Hand in hand, they continued to descend, down the switchbacks, through the Hermettji-Alp until they reached the tiny hamlet of Furi, where they met the rest of the climbing team. Arianna gave Tarkan a big hug and a European-style welcome kiss. They all took a cable car the rest of the way into Zermatt.

His arm locked around Arianna on the ride down, Daniel realized he had found the answer to the question he posed to himself earlier that afternoon. Attaining the summit of the Matterhorn was not his real goal. It was something far more important and wonderful: the true love he had known for years had finally found him, the greatest gift the world could ever give.

EPILOGUE

Seattle

By the time Daniel returned to his business in Seattle, he discovered its financing problems had disappeared. Linda Kane greeted him with a big hug and related the story of how, during Daniel's absence, their bank officer and its president paid a surprise visit to her and Peter Reed. The bank offered them a line of credit three times that of the company's current needs for the next two years. And to help finance an international expansion, a special package was included, that linked an affiliate bank in Switzerland with a letter of credit program virtually guaranteeing a financing arrangement for any European or Asian customer's order.

Capricorn Solutions, LLC, its customers, vendors, employees, and owners were positioned to flourish for years to come.

Daniel had made three trips to Turkey to assist the Secretary of State in reaching her goals

And in the U.S., at the President's request, Daniel made dozens of appearances at Rotary Clubs, conventions, and large political gatherings, touting the administration's programs to help small businesses gain better financing.

Of course his speeches were always followed by an avalanche of questions from an admiring public about surviving the hijacking and landing the Karaca Airlines 767 aircraft.

Still to come was his anticipated visit to Russia as part of his promise to Prime Minister Putin, whose staff was busy scheduling appearances with Russian audiences desperate to meet the man who protected their vital energy-production facilities. Their appreciation became more acute as the Russian winter began its relentless assault. But that is a story for another time.

EDITOR ACKNOWLEDGMENT

Christina N. Dudley   *The Book Coach*

An accomplished author in her own right, Christina was able to bring this neophyte writer into the twenty first century literary world kicking, screaming, …and laughing. This was no small feat considering she was working with an entrenched technocrat who's only writing experience consisted of business plans and performance reviews. I'll always remember her amazing ability to keep an eye on the story line at the same time as performing hundreds of detailed edits. She is one of those special people who embody the phrase: *Whatever is worth doing is worth doing well.* Thanks to her this story actually became publishable.

ACKNOWLEDGMENTS

A number of people and organizations have assisted me in creating this story and bringing it to print. Without their help the publication of this book would not have been possible. They are listed here alphabetically by last name.

Ed Anders. Ed's many years of experience as a movie stuntman and stunt coordinator provided the author with the basis for a major action scene toward the end of the story.

John Balcerak. I'm grateful to John for much needed assistance in plot development and background research.

Richard M. Farnell. Appreciation is in order for the work performed by my brother in reviewing early stages of the book and his insights on piloting a light aircraft.

Carolyn Hess. An avid reader, Carolyn was a great sounding board for plot development. Her review comments were much appreciated.

Kiros. The Bellevue, WA chapter of this organization has continually encouraged me to follow my dream during my transition from a career as a chief financial officer to becoming a creative writer. www.kiros.org.

Aida Koujumjian. The author of *Between the Two Rivers* convinced this left-brained writer he could create a love story, even when he refused to believe he had the skills to do so. info@coffeetownpress.com

Shirley Kinsey. A teacher and great proof-reader, Shirley helped me streamline my writing style.

Linda Krippaehne. Linda helped me with plot and character development and provided valuable feedback reviewing an intermediate stage of the book.

Sara Larson. Principal of Sara Larson Design, the creator of the graphics for this book's cover. Sara's research for mesmerizing images and media savvy motivated me to develop a broader vision of possibilities for the story's title. www.saralarsondesign.com

Joan Niehaus. Joan's support for me as I developed this story revealed her remarkable depths of wisdom and emotional intelligence, qualities exceeded only by her abundant spirit and commitment to others' well being.

Rosalind Renshaw. Also a writer with great wisdom, Rosalind gets a huge "Thank You" for her encouragement and advice.

William T. Robinson. Bill has had "boots on the ground" experience in Russia and in the Caucasus as an international attorney, advisor, and instructor. He was physically present in the Caucasus in the early 1990's and in 2003 and has made over 50 trips to various regions of Russia. He was able to set the record straight for this writer regarding the cause and effect of several political and military events in the Caucasus. www.wtrobinson.com.

Dale Schlotzhauer. An avid fiction and action reader, Dale gave me much needed feedback on plot structure and reminders to 'stay on the trail' with my writing style.

Timothy T. Weber, Ph.D. Tim's expert lectures and publications on family of origin concepts inspired the addition of several themes to this book's major characters. www.saybrook.edu

Hamza Yildiz. My prime connection to the exotic city of Istanbul. Hamza coached me through several iterations of Turkish phrases for this book and proved to be an invaluable guide on my first visit to the city where east meets west. www.seeingisdreaming.com/

ABOUT THE AUTHOR

After completing his MBA at Syracuse University, Douglas W. Farnell served as Chief Financial Officer for several small businesses through the 2008 financial crisis and its multi-year aftermath. That period of upheaval inspired this work, as did his pursuit of summits, which has taken him from the North Cascades  to the Rockies and Alps, as well as to Europe, Asia, and Central America.

Farnell makes his home in Seattle, where he volunteers as an instructor in business and finance for high-school students.

CPSIA information can be obtained
at www.ICGtesting.com
Printed in the USA
FFHW022331260919
55239163-60984FF